A CHRISTMAS WISH

CHERYL BARTON

Published by: Cheryl Barton Publishing, LLC
This book is a work of fiction and any references or similarities to actual events, real people, living or dead, or to real places, are intended to give the novel a sense of reality. Any similarities in names, characters, places and incidents are entirely coincidental.

For permission requests, write to the publisher, addressed to: "Attention: Permissions Coordinator," at the email address below.

Cheryl Barton Publishing, LLC
prez@crbarton.com

Ordering Information:
Quantity sales.
Special discounts of this novel are available on quantity purchases by corporations, associations, and others. For details, contact the publisher at the address above. For orders by U.S. trade bookstores and wholesalers, please contact prez@crbarton.com

ISBN-13: 978-1-948950-59-6

Dedication

To my father and mother, John and Barbara Barton, for making sure my brothers and I grew up in a house with many happy Christmases full of love and wonderful memories. To the toys under the tree, the cookies left for Santa, live trees every year and the Christmas morning family breakfast – it was everything we could ever wish for and more.

Thank you for setting the bar high on happiness and love.

Also by Cheryl Barton
www.cherylbarton.net
**Coming Soon*

Bachelor Series
Bachelor Not for Sale
A Designed Affair
A Perfect Combination
Love at Last
**Twelve Bachelors for Sale*

A Lovers' Heart Series
Heartthrob
Heartbeat
Heartbreaker

Brothers of Chi-Town Series
I Can't Let Go, 1
Swagger and Baggage, 2
Claiming His Child, 3
Always Bet on Black, 4
It Takes Two to Tangle, 5
Crashing Into Love, 6
**Leaks, Lies, Lust and Love, 7*

Malibu Hearts Series
And Then There Was You

Sister Act Series
**An Unexpected Destiny*
**For You I Will*
**More Than Friends*

The Sullivans of Montana
Home for Thanksgiving, Book 1
The Way You Love Me, Book 2
**On the Right Track, Book 3*

Game Changers
**On the Lam*

Stand Alone Romance

Snowbound
Cupid's Arrow
One Wish
His Halloween Promise
Holly for Christmas
A Better Man
Bossy
Un-Break My Heart
Love on Top
Take a Knee
Love at First Sight
My First Love
Black Love
A Younger Man
The Lake House
True Lies or True Love
When I Think of You
Seize the Moment
Baby Come Back
Unforgettable
**It Should Have Been You*
**Christmas in Vermont*
**The Christmas Layover*

1

"Look, William, it's that nice fire captain from the fire station in our community," Lillian Halston said.

William Halston looked to where his wife of fifty years was pointing and sure enough, there was Captain Kenneth Gibson, Harford County, Maryland's best and fiercest fireman and from what he'd heard, one of the most eligible bachelors according to county chatter about him. Together they looked his way and smiled while he perused the numerous Christmas trees on the lot of their Christmas shop. This wasn't the first year the captain had come for a tree, usually finding the perfect one for him and his daughter. Today, William noticed that the captain looked more indecisive than usual. He also realized there was something different in his wife's voice that told him her comment wasn't a casual one. She wasn't just unintentionally noticing him. William knew what was coming next. He smiled, as he did every year, when he heard her all-too familiar tone and he was ready to play along, as he always has.

"It sure is him, isn't it? I don't see that little sweetheart daughter of his. She has the prettiest name; Willow. Christmas time every year, when she's with him, she runs right over to give us a hug and tells us how excited she is to help her dad decorate for the holiday. I wonder where she is this year?" he said.

"Why don't you go over and say hello to him. Maybe you can ask him that yourself. He looks to be alone this year, again, and quite puzzled by the look on his face. We have more trees than usual this year, yet he looks like he can't decide on a tree. I bet he's still single, though I bet, if interested, he would have his pick of women. If he's here all by himself, I guess he still hasn't found that perfect love like we have had all these years," Lillian said.

She gave her husband a certain look, knowing he knew the meaning behind it.

William fell for it just like he had every year leading up to this one. He usually went along with her plan, but there was something about the way the captain looked that said this may not be the year for him. Perhaps, for the first time, his Lillian was wrong about her vision.

"No, Lillian. We can't do that. I usually agree, but maybe this isn't the year for him."

"Well, why not? What makes you think if I feel that it's him and perhaps you don't, that I'm not right? There have been some years that you've felt that way and yet, years after, we still get Christmas cards and gifts from couples thanking us for their tree. It was done for us and haven't we been happy since day one? Why can't we help him out?"

"I usually get a feeling that the person you set your eyes on would be a believer. Something is missing about the captain. Maybe it's me. I don't know. How do we know he will even make a wish?"

Looking at Lillian, he saw that impatient look in her eyes. He was the doubter between the two of them.

"It doesn't have to be him that makes the wish. It just has to be done to the right tree and we both know which tree that is," Lillian replied.

Not convinced, William questioned her again.

"How do we know anyone around him will make the kind of wish that's needed? If his heart isn't open to it, we know it's not going to work. He seems to be happy being a single man. A lot of people are, you know. Not everyone thinks their life would be perfect being married. Besides, he was married before and it didn't work out."

"That's because the right wish wasn't made on the right tree. We didn't know him back then and he didn't start coming to us for his tree until the year he divorced."

"Lillian, we're supposed to be specific about the tree. Only one tree grows a year and we have to be careful and sure," he said.

William felt himself caving in. He knew it was the spirit of Christmas that was coming over him that would, in a few more sentences, send him over to his wife's way of the force.

"We've sold the one tree that grows on that lot every year since you purchased our tree that year, fifty years ago. You were a true believer after finding out one tree grew for the purpose of making love last forever. And then, that next year, it wasn't a coincidence that Mr. Shepherd offered to sell us his Christmas shop, including that tree that grew every year in the back of the building. Every year since then, we have sold the tree to the right person. That's forty-nine years of someone finding their happy ever after following the year we found ours. Look at the that number of wishes being granted. Everyone we've sold those trees to made the wish. It's the tree and you know it. No one can resist making a wish once they encounter the tree after it's cut down. We're retiring after this Christmas season, which means we have to sell the last one. I think Captain Gibson is more than worthy of it. You thought he should have had it last year when he showed up with that awful girl he was dating. I had a dream that he wasn't going to last with her and I was right. He has the purest heart, would give his last to anyone and we both know he would make the perfect husband."

"He was married before," William offered.

"There wasn't a wish made on the tree for love to last for him. It's his time."

William glanced at the man again as he browsed the many trees available.

"He's not even looking for a tree that tall. Look, he's

looking through the eight-foot trees," he offered cheerfully.

When the captain turned and looked their way, they waved together.

"Merry Christmas, Captain!" Lillian hollered.

"Merry Christmas!" he replied.

"It's him," Lillian exclaimed. "You needed a sign, there it was," she added.

"He's still not looking at the tall trees," he said.

"You know it must be the eleven-foot tree in the back."

William watched Lillian as she moved about the outside of the shop adjusting flowers and other décor items like she didn't have a care in the world. She was so sure of herself. That was one of a million things he loved about her. When she knew, she knew.

"What if his house isn't big enough for a tree that tall?"

"William, when have you ever doubted my vision? Think about this – I'm not usually here this early in the day with you, but I was up extra early, dressed, and ready to go. I knew today was the day. The minute I saw him, I knew."

"Who is the woman?" William inquired. "There is usually a woman in your vision."

Lillian smiled sly-like.

"Oh, there is. I'll tell you about her later. You're going to be a doubter this time, for sure."

"Am I?"

"Yes. You're going to tell me that I'm crazy thinking they will make the perfect match. It will happen, but the tree is the key. You know I'm right. I have been for the past forty-nine years and this year is no different, as I've already told you. Think of all the beautiful families we've had a hand in creating. We were given the gift of the tree and we've done a great job making sure we do the job right. This is our last year and our last tree. It belongs to Captain Gibson. You go on over and convince him right now that he should get that taller tree. I already know he has the space for it. The tree knows too."

"You're going to say it, aren't you?" William asked.

Lillian winked at him and he knew it was coming.

"I sure am. *Santa Claus* is waiting to hear from us that we've found another perfect recipient of the tree. You know what it's like when I get that feeling. I woke up this morning knowing that the next person to get the tree would arrive today. I didn't know it was him until I turned around and saw him."

"You're sure it's him?" William asked.

"Stop it. I'm positive. Go do your part. I pick them out and you convince them to get the tree."

William slipped on his gloves, pulled the collar of his down jacket up around his neck while pulling his wool cap down over his ears. The morning was blistering cold, but never too cold when it came to the recipient of the tree.

"Our last and final tree," he said.

"It's been an incredible ride and I can't think of anyone else, right now, who deserves the kind of perfection in love like we have. He's ready."

"What about the woman?"

"She doesn't know it yet, but she's ready too. They are like night and day, but do you know what the perfect night and day makes?" Lillian offered.

"What?"

"It makes for the perfect combination; a complete day, every single day consisting of overflowing, everlasting, unconditional love. And you know what? The key to all of this is going to be his little girl."

"The child? Have we ever had that? Have we ever had a child making a wish on the tree about love? I know we get toys and other child-like things, but you're talking about a wish for love."

"No, but maybe this is the year for something new."

"My love, are you going to miss the make-a-wish tree sale after this final year?"

William knew he was going to miss it but it was time to pass this magical gift on to another person to accomplish in the next fifty years what he and Lillian had accomplished for the past forty-nine, fifty including this year.

"Not when I can look out into the world and see all the love we've had a hand in making. You have to convince him on the tree and then it's up to the tree to honor the wish of love, the kind that will last forever, like ours."

William grabbed some rope, knowing that for forty-nine years, he's been able to make the sale of the one tree that grows alone behind their Christmas shop.

"I'm on it, sweetheart. I hope the captain is ready," he said.

"They're both ready," Lillian said to William's back as she watched him stroll over to Captain Gibson. She smiled when only after a few seconds, the captain was following her husband to the one tree planted by Santa Claus each year to make sure a forever kind of love continues throughout the generations. What she didn't tell William was that besides selling the tree to Captain Gibson, the next person to buy and run the Christmas shop would also come by the lot today. The everlasting love they'd had a hand in the year before would be the new owners of the make-a-wish tree. Love will continue.

Turning around, she headed back into the shop, happy that a new wish was about to be granted. She so loves being Santa's helper.

2

Dressed in jeans, his favorite brown bomber leather jacket, brown gloves and hat on his head against the cold first day of December, Kenneth Gibson lifted an eleven-foot-tall Christmas tree from the flatbed of his Northsky Blue Metallic Chevrolet Silverado with as much skill as he does when he's lifting a ladder from one of the fire trucks at the firehouse where he's one of three captains. Unlike a ladder, which he feels he's mastered, the tree was giving him a run for his money. He again questioned what would possess him to allow Mr. Halston to talk him into such a humungous Christmas tree when he started out on a mission for one around seven or eight feet tall. What he hadn't thought about was how he would get the tree from the truck into the family room of his four-bedroom, four-bathroom, single family home in Harford County, a quiet suburbia area located in Maryland.

Thinking of his master plan for getting the tree

inside, he had to admit that the moment he saw it, something about it screamed that he needed to buy it. Home now with a tree this size, he should have asked a few of the guys from his firehouse to stop over to help him get it inside.

Finally getting his grip just right, thankful it was wrapped pretty tight by plastic green waxed wire, he walked toward the open garage door with the tree braced on his left shoulder when he heard a familiar voice behind him, making him smile from ear to ear and ready to forget about the tree. The voice was music to his ears. After his struggle to get the tree just right, he knew sitting it down would mean he would have to figure lifting it up again, but he had no choice. Following the voice, the next move would be a big leap into his arms and he needed to be ready.

Kenneth heard the sound of boots on the concrete racing his way as he lay the tree on the floor of his two-car garage and turned just in time to catch his nine-year-old daughter, Willow, just as her feet left the ground as she leaped, knowing he would catch her; it was their thing. When she grabbed him tight around the neck, he held her in a bear hug, delighting in how she'd just made his day. Nothing gave him more pleasure than seeing her smiling face and getting one of her much-needed hugs. His plan was to have the tree set up and ready for them to decorate later in the day when he would take the usual trip to Pennsylvania to pick her up from where she lived with her mother and step-father.

"Pumpkin, I was planning on picking you up a little later today. What are you doing here already? Not that I'm upset at all. I wanted the tree to be standing when you arrived," he said happily, placing kisses all over her cheeks.

"Daddy! Mommy brought me early. She said she tried calling you and you didn't answer. Where's your phone?" Willow asked, patting the pockets of his jacket.

"Uh, you know me. It's in the truck. I was out picking out the perfect tree and left it there. I didn't check it when I got back in. I was rushing to get the tree home and then get on the road to pick you up.

Kenneth looked beyond Willow, who was still in his arms, and at the curb in front of his house was his ex-wife, Carrie, who stepped out of her white Toyota Camry, waving so hard that her arm looked fluid, almost liquid-like in its movement.

"Hey Ken!" she hollered.

"Hey Carrie."

"I hope it's okay that I brought her to you. Dante and I were hoping to get an early start on the road to his parents in Chicago. I tried calling you," she said.

Kenneth put Willow down on her feet and walked toward her.

"Daddy! This is a big tree. Is it going to fit in the house?" Willow asked, reaching for it.

"Careful. It's prickly," he warned.

"I have gloves on," she said.

"Still, just wait for me, and yes, it will fit in the house in the family room with the high ceilings."

He then turned back to Carrie.

"You know it's never a problem anytime she needs to be here, early or late. I was out getting things ready with snacks, the tree, some extra decorations and well, food in general," he admitted.

"Still spending most of your time at the firehouse?"

"Yeah, this time of year, I like to give the team some extra hours off with family. Christmas is in a few weeks and this is a busy time of year for us."

"You're sure a month until the new year isn't too much having Willow here? I know how your schedule can be. I told her I could fly back and pick her up to give you a break, but she insisted that she be allowed to spend the entire month with you. I know what balancing kids and work can be like, especially for you, a fire captain."

"Nonsense. My folks are two blocks away, my sister and her family are three miles away, I have other family close by and Zara, the best babysitter in the world, is on standby in case of emergency."

"Ah, the perfect babysitter. Willow never stops talking about her. She showed me all the crafts they made together two weeks ago when she was here. If she was closer to me, I'd use her for Sapphire."

Kenneth looked in the car in the back where Sapphire, Carrie's daughter with her husband, Dante, would usually be in her car seat.

"Where is she? Willow told me you had a pony for Sapphire's third birthday party."

"She's home with Dante. She was sleeping and we didn't want to wake her. He knew I was coming right back. When we couldn't reach you, I called your mom to ask if I could leave Willow with her and of course, she said yes."

"You never even have to ask her that; it's always okay."

"I know, but I wanted to be sure. Willow insisted that we try you here at home first. She thought maybe you had a long night at the firehouse and that you may be home sleeping. I see you weren't. Where did you get that huge tree? Willow is going to love that."

"The Christmas shop a few miles up the highway. I still go to the same place I've always gotten the tree from. This year, I was convinced this giant of a tree was specifically for me. It grew on me the instant I saw it. Besides, it's Christmas and I love going all out for her. I'm glad she'll be here the extra time."

"I appreciate you accommodating the change in our schedule. We wouldn't usually go this early to spend Christmas with his parents but his mother is a little under the weather and he wants to get there early to set his eyes on her in person."

"No need for an explanation. I'll be praying for his mother and for you all to make it there safely."

"Thanks. Willow was so anxious to see you that she

didn't even think about her luggage in the trunk," Carrie said opening it.

Kenneth sprang into action to grab the two suitcases and two duffle bags.

"What is in these? She has as many clothes here as she does at your house."

Carrie looked for Willow and then leaned closer to him so that their daughter couldn't hear her.

"Big secret is, I gave her money to buy gifts for your whole family and she hand wrapped most of them by herself. There is more wrapping paper and tape in one of the bags. She wanted to finish the rest when she got here. She's excited!"

Kenneth laughed out loud. His little pumpkin was growing up.

"I know they're going to love them. My sister is already planning a sleepover for her girls and Willow. She's going to have fun, so don't you worry."

"Okay. Her laptop is in her backpack. She's doing online school for the last two weeks of school. I'll be back before she heads back into the classroom in January."

"Sounds like a plan. Travel safe. I better get in the house before Willow comes out complaining that she can't find any snacks," he joked.

Kenneth turned toward his house and stopped when Carrie called his name.

"Willow told me about you and Kimberly and the relationship ending and all. I'm sorry to hear that," she offered.

"Yeah, we tried to make a relationship out of what should have been a casual situation, but it's all good."

"Still, Willow liked her and you know she thinks it's past time for you to get married again."

Kenneth smiled thinking of the great relationship they still had even though they were divorced. They still talked about everything, including each other's personal lives.

"Once you remarried, she thought it was her job to try and marry me off again too. I told her if it happens, it will. It's not something that can be rushed," he explained. "She thinks I'm lonely, but I'm good."

"I love the way our little girl loves you and wants everything good for you. I'm also glad that we have always remained friends, despite our divorce."

"That's because we have always been friends, just not right for each other as husband and wife. We are also perfect parents to the perfect little girl. Her happiness and seeing us happy is what matters. Tell Dante I'm still expecting him here at my house for the Superbowl game."

"Thanks for inviting him. He told me to make sure to let you know that he would be here. Well, I'll let you go because here comes Willow with a no-snack-around-this-house, kind of look on her face," Carrie chuckled and got back in her car.

"Bye Mom!" Willow yelled.

Kenneth waved as Carrie drove off. He lifted the

luggage for her to see.

"Let's get in out of the cold. We're going to get snow for Christmas," he said.

"Yeah!" Willow jumped around. "I love snow. I packed my new snow boots. Can I get a pair of UGG boots?"

"What's that?" he asked.

"Dad! Get with the program. All the kids and stars have them. I want a pair in pink."

"Maybe Santa will bring you a pair," he suggested.

He smiled to himself that Carrie had already shared with him Willow's desire for the boots, which he'd already purchased and hidden at his sister's house.

"I put them on my list, so he knows. Just in case he's really busy and can't get them, I'm telling you and mom that I would like a pair."

"Sounds like you have all the bases covered then," he laughed.

After sitting her luggage in the garage, Kenneth, once again, lifted the tree as Willow opened and held the door open for him.

"That's why I want new boots so that I can get around in the snow."

"And still be cute, right?" he asked as they laughed together.

"Cute and warm," Willow responded and pointed him toward the door.

"That's my girl!"

"What are we going to be doing besides decorating this big tree? Do you have to work today?"

"I'm not working at the firehouse after tonight. I'm sort of on vacation, but not really. Remember I told you about the movie that's being shot here in Maryland?"

"I think so."

"With your favorite actress Bella Hardwick?"

The surprise look on Willow's face said it all. His daughter loved the twenty-eight-year-old actress who was, at the moment, the hottest and most requested actress in Hollywood. He once read that offers were coming in so fast for her that she was turning them down on a daily basis. She was happy to be in such demand that she could pick and choose the movies that worked for her.

"Dad! Are you serious? She's the biggest action star in the world. She has moves that are better than Trinity from the Matrix movies. I heard they even want her to be in the next Matrix movie if she's available. She's going to rock at that if she does. You know how we do."

Kenneth laughed at her lingo.

"How we do? Where did you pick that up?"

"Some show. It means black women can do any and everything they set their minds to. I like what it means. Isn't that what you tell me all the time?"

She listens, he thought and silently patted himself on the back.

"You know it! You will be all you want to be because your mindset will be that you can. I'm glad you remembered that."

"I like saying it. What about this movie she's in? What does it have to do with you?" she asked.

"They need firemen on the set while certain scenes are being shot and I was recruited. It was supposed to be one of the other captains at my firehouse, but he hates doing those type of things. I was already scheduled to be off through the end of the year, unless I get called in for an emergency. This is my first real vacation off this whole year and I knew you were coming for the whole month. Guess what? On some days, I may be able to bring you to the set. Wouldn't that be exciting? You always say you want to be a Hollywood movie director one day."

Kenneth set the tree up in the stand he'd already put in place beside the fireplace and in front of the large floor to ceiling window that overlooked the large expanse which was the back of his property which was enclosed by a six-foot, white privacy fence. He was waiting to hear cheers from Willow, but hearing nothing, he turned around to find her in a trance, not moving, not talking – just staring at him as if she were looking at a ghost. He waited, walked toward her, smiling while waving his hands across her face.

"Dad are you joking? If so, that's a terrible joke."

"It's not a joke. I wouldn't joke about your favorite actress."

"This is so exciting! Would I get to meet her?"

"I don't know. Maybe I could arrange it, but no

promises."

"That's officially all I want for Christmas, dad. You have to let me meet her, please!"

Kenneth chuckled so hard, his whole body moved. He loved seeing her this enthusiastic.

"I will see what I can do. I'll be working, so I'll have responsibilities. I have to keep the set safe along with a few others hired for the duration. Now, how about you come back down to earth and help me get the food and snacks from the car."

"If you let me meet her, I will keep my room cleaned forever and ever. I promise I will. She is my favorite actress and you know it. She's your favorite actress too. Do you think she's pretty?" Willow asked.

Kenneth knew what was coming next.

"Yes, she's very pretty."

"I think so too. You could ask her out, you know, and then I could meet her. Wouldn't that be nice? We would both be happy."

"I'm not going to ask her out. I will be there working, not looking for a date."

"You should though."

"Willow, we've talked about this. I do not need to be dating anyone. You don't like spending all of your time with just me?" he asked, adding a sad look to his face.

"Yes, you do. You need a girlfriend. When I'm home with mom and Dante, you're here all alone or at the firehouse with all the other men. Don't you want a new wife? Mom found a new husband."

"No, not at this moment. I'm fine and trust me, I don't need my nine-year-old-daughter on the lookout for a woman for me."

"I liked Ms. Kim, but she wasn't the right girlfriend for you. You should have a girlfriend like Bella Hardwick. She would be the perfect step-mom. We could go to all the Hollywood parties and I can meet all my favorite actors. That would be fun. Did you get popcorn?" Willow asked.

Kenneth shook his head at how easily Willow could change a subject.

"I did. I have some in the bag and I bought some we can pop. I finally got that popcorn machine set up in the theater room downstairs."

He leaned down to let her see what was in one of the bags he carried.

"Can we watch a movie and pop some popcorn tomorrow night since you have to work tonight?"

"I'm thinking we'll order pizza, some wings and yes, pop some popcorn and if we can stay awake long enough, there is ice cream and a box of cones in one of these bags."

"You think of everything, dad. If you had a girlfriend, like say, Bella, we could invite her over to watch with us."

"She's twenty-eight years old and I'm thirty-six. She wouldn't have any interest in an everyday, ordinary run of the mill guy like me who is that much older than her. She's a super star actress and I'm a firefighter. She can have any man she wants. Besides, I think she has a boyfriend, that Brandon guy."

"I don't like him, dad. I know you don't let me on social media yet, but I hear from my friends that he's not a good boyfriend to her."

"That may be the case, but still, he is her boyfriend which means she is taken."

"You're a hottie, dad. All my friends' moms say it. They think their kids don't hear them but they think you are a handsome hottie. Bella will think so too if you ask her out. You should have a girlfriend. Molly in my class – I heard her mom ask my music teacher if you would be coming to the Valentine's Day assembly in February because she wanted to get another look at how you walk and then she whistled. Why would she want to see you walk?"

"Willow!"

"I know, I know. I need to stay out of grown people business. I'm just saying. I want you to be happy like mommy is."

"I am happy. You make me happy and that's all I need in my life. You, me, movies and popcorn. I even planning a marathon of all of the Star Wars movies."

"Yeah!" Willow shouted while running back into the house.

Leaving the first group of supermarket bags on the floor of the garage, Kenneth went back out to his truck and waved to Yolanda, one of his neighbors who was newly separated from her husband. He knew it wasn't random that she mysteriously shows up outside of her house every time he's outside of his. He waved when she used all ten of her long, manicured nails to wave at him. He inwardly shook his head at her coming out of her house in bootie shorts and a tank top, no bra covering her gigantic enhancements and high-heeled pink shoes. The temperature was just above ten degrees. She was well under-dressed and he knew why, but he wasn't biting. He's seen enough men sneaking in and out of her house at all hours of the day and night, even one of their neighbors who was married. He wanted none of that, but he was always cordial.

"Hey there, Ms. Yolanda! Beautiful weather we're having, isn't it?" he shouted with humor.

"It is pretty warm for a winter day. I see Willow is here."

"Yes, she's here through the end of the year."

"Big plans for the holiday?" she asked.

"Spending some much-needed daddy and daughter time with my princess. What about you?"

He asked but didn't really want to know.

"I'll get into something. My ex has the kids and I'm happy. I need a break from them. If you need me to sit for Willow, I'm free anytime for you. All you have to do is knock on my door. I'm always home."

"Yeah, you get enough knocks on your door," Kenneth said under his breath.

"I'll keep that in mind," he finally said to her before

heading back into the garage, this time, closing the door down behind him.

"She's nasty."

Kenneth saw Willow standing in the door between the kitchen and the garage. He coughed to keep himself from laughing. He didn't want Willow to think it was okay to say that, but it was funny.

With a straight face, he turned to her.

"Willow, that's not nice."

"It's what mom says about her. I heard her once tell Dante, that she was nasty. What does that mean?" she asked.

Kenneth exhaled, happy that Willow didn't already know what the reference meant, though he did.

"Don't worry about it. Don't let me hear you say that about her or anyone else again. Just stay away from her house."

Following her into the house, Kenneth's mind turned to Bella Hardwick when he looked down on the counter at the packet of information he received regarding the plan for him being on set. He was to work along with the hired crew to be sure there were no fire hazards on the set of Bella's new action flick. He looked forward to being a part of the safety crew.

In his daughter's presence, he tried to play down his obvious attraction to the beautiful actress who reminded him of another very beautiful actress, Zoe Saldana. People have often made claims that the two actresses had to be twins separated at birth because they looked that much alike. The only difference is that Bella's natural hair color was a dark reddish brown which matched her hazel eye color perfectly.

The first time he saw Bella in a movie was her first major feature four years ago, *The Night Watch*. The movie turned out to be the major action blockbuster movie of the year which was huge for a first feature for an actress. She had done other roles in television shows and some small movie roles, but that was her first time as the star and she had knocked that role out of the park. Since then, she's played in three other huge hits, all hitting the number one spot and her being named the most versatile actress Hollywood has seen in a long time. Many compare her actions to those of Angelina Jolie. Bella could do it all, but she shined best when she was kicking butt in her movies.

The movie she was currently shooting in Maryland had her playing an ex-CIA agent who seeks revenge on a major spy ring who found out her identity and came after her family, killing her fiancé. The last part of the movie takes place after she settles back in the Maryland/D.C. area. As an agent, she didn't realize that one threat still remains from someone on her own team who turned out to be a double agent.

Kenneth was happy that he was around the day his chief asked if anyone was interested in providing support when the other captain backed out. Everyone was interested, but he was selected, since it was preferred that someone in a leadership position be used. Being off for most of the month was beneficial since his absence at the firehouse was already planned for. He held in his excitement of hopefully being able to meet her and then telling Willow about it. They often watched her movies over and over again with as much joy as if they were watching them for the first time.

Bella was definitely a man's dream beauty and from what he could tell from several interviews, she had a beautiful heart and spirit to go along with her good looks. What he didn't admire was her choice of men.

Like a lot of men and women in her line of work, her dating life appeared to exist around those in the industry with her. There were a few professional athletes thrown in, none of which were truly worthy of her, but it wasn't for him to judge. He struggled through his own relationships that didn't go well, some his fault, some not.

Unlike Willow, he didn't see himself going out on a date with Bella, though he wouldn't shy away from the idea. He didn't think she'd go for an average guy when she could have a superstar like herself as a partner. She certainly deserved someone who would appreciate her for who she was. That was not her current boyfriend, according to news reports. Brandon was a playboy. If he knew it, Bella had to know it as well. Perhaps, that was the kind of man she desired. If that was the case, he was far from the type of guy she would like. Women were meant to be cherished and respected; not used and abused simply for some man's ego.

Still, he was looking forward to tomorrow, his first day on the movie set.

"Come on, dad! I'm starving. Can we have hotdogs before you leave? Is Kara coming over later when you have to work? I ate breakfast but nothing for lunch."

"Yes, we can and no, Kara isn't coming tonight. You're going to Aunt Lindsay's house for a sleepover tonight with your cousins. It's my last shift tonight, so I'll be by to pick you up sometime tomorrow, late in the day. I have to be on set tomorrow for most of the day."

"Yippee! I love going to Aunt Lindsay's house. Mom helped me pick out some stuff to make a gingerbread house. Maybe we can do that while I'm at her house?" she asked.

"I'm sure everyone will love that. Like Kara, Aunt Lindsay loves doing all kinds of crafty stuff with you and your cousins."

"I'll make sure to take it with me."

"We can eat lunch and then you can help me pull out the decorations so that we can see what else we'll need. You also need to get your luggage unpacked and then pack a bag since you're going for tonight."

"I can't wait to see Aunt Lindsay. She's married and happy right?" Willow added and Kenneth gave her the side-eye.

"Really?" he asked and then smiled.

"I know, dad. You want me to stay out of grown people stuff. I'll open the hotdogs."

Kenneth already knew he was about to have an interesting couple of weeks leading up to Christmas. There was never a dull moment with his feisty daughter around. He wouldn't have it any other way. He had a feeling this Christmas was going to be one of their best yet. He looked over at the tree and though he wanted to deny the big tree was for him, it looked perfect in his home. It was as if the tree was specifically made just for his family room. He would need to pull out the ladder for this one and definitely get more decorations. There was something about Christmas that made him feel like a kid again, especially having Willow with him. He was more than ready to get the holiday started off right.

He looked back down at the packet on the counter and his thoughts turned back to Bella. He wondered what she was like face-to-face. He smiled knowing he would soon find out.

3

Hair aficionado, Desiree Barksdale curled hair, fluffed hair and then curled some more before losing her grip on Bella's hair each time she turned her head to converse with others who were also in the star's trailer. She had been doing Bella's hair since her first acting gig when she was nineteen years old.

They had been best friends since their elementary school days back in North Carolina. The moment Bella stepped into her new role as an actress, her first requirement was that her best friend be added to her team to do her hair for everything from television and movie roles to talk show appearance. Right now, she was losing her patience with her best friend and how she could not keep her head still.

Not only was she moving her head depending on who she as talking to, but Bella was also dancing around in her chair to the Christmas music that played throughout the trailer. She knew her friend loved this time of year and until the taping of the movie wrapped up in a few weeks, right before Christmas, there would be holiday music every day. She would have to deal with the dancing actress as she tried to steady her hand, until then.

"Bella, I swear, if you don't stop moving, you're going to need make-up to cover the burn spot on your face. You are one head turn away from a flat iron to your forehead," Desiree chastised.

She planted a hand on her hip while raising the flat iron in the air, sucking her teeth and smacking hard on some of the best strawberry bubble gum she'd ever tasted.

"Gum smacking? Really?" Bella asked. "What is it with you and bubble gum. I see those wrappers all over the place!"

"You know how I get in the morning. I need that sugar rush and y'all stopped me from drinking coffee because it made me extra, extra, so bubble gum it is. Turn and look in the mirror and tell me what you think? The scene for this afternoon is in the deli where you're having lunch after leaving a spa day with one of your friends. You spot the traitor out on the street and you pull your long curls up into a ponytail holder from your wrist so that you can put a hat on and follow him. How do you like this long, flowing look? The hat will mess it up, but you will look dynamic before that."

Bella turned left, right and then left again, twirling her head, dancing with happiness in the chair. She checked to make sure the curls weren't too stiff. She loved that she was able to use her own naturally long hair and not one of those stuffy wigs she sometimes had to have. She could do a better job of putting it up and taking it down without worrying if the seams on the wig would show.

"I love everything about this look. You know how I normally like my hair down anyway. This way, one quick swoop and it's up. This is perfect!" Bella exclaimed.

"Five more minutes Bella!" one of the production assistants hollered into her trailer after opening the door and closing it right back. Today they were doing a dry run of the scene along with a fiery crash that happens as a result of an explosion. In that scene, she's thrown backwards, or her stunt double, River, is thrown backwards, just out of reach of the blast. She still had to be in the scene until the crash and then they would switch her out for River.

"I'll be right there," she replied and hopped out of the chair where she'd just gotten her hair and makeup done.

"Oh, wait. Let me warn you about something," Desiree whispered out of earshot of everyone else gathered around chatting. She pulled Bella to the side for a more intimate conversation.

"What's up?"

"Well, when I got here you were already in the makeup chair, so you didn't see this fine brother on the set working the fire safety angle today. I'm telling you, when I saw him, like every other woman, and probably most of the men on the set, my mouth went dry – I mean all the moisture dissipated. He's an actual, real-life fireman and all I can say is, I wouldn't mind being rescued by him at all! Picture this; Will Smith's fine ass in that movie, *Hitch*. I won't tell anyone how you foam at the mouth over that brother, especially all of his quality man meat in that movie and the *Bad Boy* movies with Martin Lawrence. This fireman is all things Will Smith including the walk. Now you know how we are about that man's walk. This guy – wait until you see him. Girl, you are in for a real treat."

Bella waved Desiree's comment off and checked herself one last time in the mirror.

"Not likely. I have a man and a very fine one, thank you very much. Are we having drinks this evening? We have an early shoot tomorrow morning, so any idea of going out is off the table, but we can open up a bottle in my hotel suite. I'm going to need a serious wind-down later."

Desiree snapped her fingers in Bella's face as if she needed to be brought back to life.

"I know you did not just toss out my comment all flippant like and changed it to drinks. I'm warning you – I don't care what your man looks like, this guy is the best eye candy I've ever seen. Don't get me started on Brandon and what I think about you still claiming him as your man. You know how he does. Speaking of your *man* that you want to act like is walking on water in your world, I assume he had an explanation for the latest on him cheating on you while on his latest movie set in Paris?"

"Not true," Bella immediately defended. She was also lying. She tried to keep a happy face when it came to Brandon, but he was making a fool out of her. He had a problem keeping his zipper up and secure around just about any woman he encountered. His latest antics in Paris didn't escape her. She played her unhappiness off as she always had. She also hadn't told anyone that she and Brandon weren't really as much of an item as they had been. He couldn't be trusted and she was tired of being walked all over and teased like she had to put up with him; she didn't.

If only she could reveal her true feelings to those around her. She could to Desiree, but there were too many others in the room and she didn't need anyone seeing her sweating over yet another actor cheating on her. Even though Desiree tried to whisper, Bella could see that all other talk in the room had ended as they waited for her reaction.

"Really? That's what you're going with?" Desiree asked.

"Brandon already called me and said the photo was altered."

"Bella! Are you serious right now? You know that man has a community penis," Desiree whispered.

All eyes were on her now as the idea of Brandon

doing to her the same as he's been doing the entire time they've been in a relationship came to the surface. She saw the looks of pity focused on her and she needed space.

"Everybody out!" Bella yelled.

The trailer quickly emptied out. When she and Desiree were alone, she flopped back into the makeup chair, lowing her head in her hands.

"It's real, isn't it?" Desiree questioned.

"Yes. Why can't he stop falling into the closest snatch? I'm so sick of it. I ended the relationship. My publicist told me to not say anything about it until the movie is about to come out. They're hoping to build on the hype for the movie with personal drama and Brandon surely does bring plenty of that."

"Stop it! You're letting them use your personal relationship tragedy to sell more movie tickets?"

Bella looked up at her childhood friend, one of several members of her team that she required whenever she signed a contract. She had to bring along her own makeup, hair and clothing designer, all friends from back home. Desiree did her hair, Dana was her makeup artist and Shelton was her clothing designer who kept her looking good at all times, on and off set. They have all been friends since their high school days at the school for the arts. They never lost touch.

Bella happily reached back to friends in Raleigh she knew were trying to break into the industry. Where she went on movie sets and other appearances, they went with her. All were well known and were often requested by other stars. She didn't mind as long as the look they gave others didn't match hers in any way.

"I know I shouldn't, but I look forward to dragging Brandon's cheating behind through the mud. For now, it's all Hollywood politics and you know how that goes. He's cheated on me more times than I can count and I've always taken him back to keep my image intact."

"Girl, your image has nothing to do with him. You know you don't have to have a superstar to be somebody? Remember that old song you love that goes, *"you don't have to be a star baby, to be in my show*?"

Bella smiled at the revelation.

"One of my favorite old songs by Marilyn McCoo & Billy Davis, Jr. I grew up on my father playing that song over and over for my mother."

"There is some truth to that. You're always chasing after the next guy who has as much as you so that you wouldn't have to worry that he was out for your money and not for you. What you end up with is a guy who uses his street credibility of bedding Bella Hardwick so that he can get other women. Yeah, Brandon is a star in his own right, but that doesn't mean he gets to treat you like a play thing when he wants to, while flaunting other women in your face. He knows cameras are always on him. The latest is of him hooking up in the back of a limousine with some woman. I think I actually saw the image of a second woman in the photos."

"I know. He tried to claim it wasn't him at first until

TMZ came up with a copy of the video that the girl set up with her cellphone when Brandon was busy taking her skirt off. Not only did the video catch his voice, but it caught his face just as he was about to plant it between her two huge mounds. Pisses me off that he did that knowing it could get out."

"He keeps doing that. When do you stop accepting it?" Desiree asked.

Feeling empowered that she took the right step to end things, Bella stood up, checked her makeup and let go of the pain of yet another man treating her like dirt.

"I have stopped. I'm not taking him back again. I'm done and giving up on men. Maybe I'll find me a good woman like you did."

"Stop playing like that. You are all about that male appendage and not just that, but also the fact that he's all male. I love Asha, but a woman is not for you. I always knew I would love a woman and six months after meeting Asha, I made her my wife. It's been three of the best years of my life. She completes me. She loves me. She respects me. I love her. I adore her. We fit together. You need a man who is all of those things for you and you for him. Your mess with Brandon is one-sided. Do you know what is for you?"

Desiree smiled glibly.

"What?"

"A sexier than sexy fireman. Wait until you see him. He showed up in a bomber jacket, looking like something in a biker boy dream. The legs – I can't even describe the legs to you. Did I mention he has on jeans that cup his butt just right? Even I found him attractive and that's a rarity for me. I was unable to look away and you and I both know I've only been about women since high school. This brother? I'd let him hit it!" Desiree yelled and they doubled over in laughter together.

"Okay, I guess I really need to see this guy after that description, and from you of all people. He looks that good, huh?"

"Let me tell it to you like this; once you see him, you're going to be asking Santa to put a bow around him and place him under your tree on Christmas morning. I would stake my next pay check on it."

"Bet?" Bella asked.

Now, she was intrigued.

"Bet and a half!" Desiree declared boldly.

"Let's get a look at him then."

"I have a question for you. What are you going to do about Christmas now that you say you've broken up with Brandon? You were going to join him in Paris for the holiday week between then and New Year's Day after the final day of shooting the few days before Christmas."

"I don't know. I sent my parents on a trip to Bali until the new year, so that's out. I don't want to go there and end up a third wheel. My brother and his wife went to stay at my new condo in Hawaii. They're planning to do Christmas and stay through the new year. I don't want to crash that either. I guess I'll head to my place in Los Angeles. What are you and Asha doing?"

"We decided that this year we aren't visiting family or having anyone over. We want to relax and enjoy each other. You already know that we're thinking about using a surrogate to have a baby next year, so we want to enjoy this time before life gets crazy with a baby. Also, I've been on the road for the past year with you on the various sets for this movie and even though Asha was able to join me on a lot of these trips, I want to relax with her in my arms and do nothing for an entire week, maybe two. I'm working on a new television show that starts filming in mid-January. You'll have a lot of time before you start your press run before the movie is released late next year. What are you going to do? Just sit at home alone?"

Bella didn't want to respond that she didn't have any other choice. She either reached out in desperation to Brandon or some other ex to spend the holidays with or she relented and spent it wishing on a star that the next holiday season would be better than this one and the last one. Last year hadn't turned out the way she had hoped either. She was tired of the fast, Hollywood lifestyle. She would love to resort back to the kind of holiday she grew up having – quiet, opening gifts, food and movies. She wanted a chance to relax with no parties or hosting on the agenda; definitely not for the cameras. She missed quiet holidays with her family around the fireplace.

"I don't know. I want you to have a great holiday.

You know I love you and Asha. I have gifts for you both before you leave the set to go back home. Make sure we connect beforehand."

"I want my gift now!" Desiree joked.

"I know you do, but not until the last day on-set. You're more anxious than a little kid on Christmas morning. I love the anticipation!"

"Whatever. Let's go look at the meat market that has arrived; one particular portion, to be exact. If you don't find him attractive, drinks tonight are on me and I know you like that expensive stuff."

"That's a deal. What would I do with a fireman in Maryland?"

"Get you a good hose!" Desiree quipped.

They laughed and tripped as they exited the trailer. Before she could gather herself, Bella found herself struggling for balance before falling on her knees. She was happy she hadn't fallen on her face. She started to get up when a strong pair of hands lifted her as if she were as light as a feather. After wiping her pants off, she stood to her full, five-foot-eight height and came face to face with a god-like Adonis with a grave look of concern on his handsome face. Had she ever seen a man this handsome before? She wasn't sure. Seeing him took her breath away and she was stunned into silence.

"Are you alright? Are you hurt?" he asked.

Words. Bella needed words, but none came to mind. She was too busy being happily distracted by the man who just saved her from sheer embarrassment.

Did he just ask her a question? What did she miss? Bella couldn't comprehend or speak. Her lips or her tongue wouldn't move. It lay like cement in her mouth when her eyes gathered on the best-looking man she'd ever seen; there was no doubt about that. Noting the bomber jacket and the fact that he was a Will Smith look-a-like, she turned to Desiree for help. She couldn't get her mouth to work for nothing.

"Uh, she looks like she's okay. She may need a lint roller, but this is only a dry-run and not what she'll be wearing for the actual scene. Bella, you're good, right?"

She was thankful for the few seconds Desiree had bought her. Bella turned her eyes back to the man in front of her and gulped loudly cursing her tongue for defying her. She finally found her words.

"I'm good, thanks to you for lifting me up a second after I fell," she stammered out.

"Yeah, that left me to fend for myself," Desiree joked.

"I'm sorry. I was closest to Ms. Hardwick. I tried reaching for you just now, but you were already standing," Kenneth explained. "Are you alright?"

When she nodded, Kenneth turned his attention back to Bella and she again, marveled at her instant reaction to him; a first for her. He looked good, he sounded sexy with a deep, melodious, almost southern drawl and to top it off, he smelled delicious with a woodsy, musk, all-man scent.

"It's no trouble. I guess we were laughing too hard and forgot there was a little step at the bottom of the stairs to her trailer," Desiree admitted.

"You're sure?" he asked.

"We are. You are?" Desiree asked.

Bella was so embarrassed. Desiree was engaging the man the way she should be. She felt left out because she was overwhelmed by the feeling of bursting at the seam with desire for the perfect specimen before her.

"I'm Kenneth Gibson, local firefighter and hired hand to check out all fire hazards for the shoots for the next week, maybe beyond, depending on the need," he said.

"Need?" Bella finally said. That one word did more for her than any other word in the English dictionary could do.

When he looked at her puzzled over her one-word question, she finally found her common sense.

"She may be a little discombobulated from the fall. You're definitely needed around here. That's what she meant to say," Desiree noted.

Bella was glad, again, that her bestie had stepped in and saved the day. All she could think was that she wasn't thinking that at all. Her body was having all kinds of other ideas of what the word *'need'* meant to her. Looks like Desiree wasn't going to lose the bet this time and Bella was happy about it.

"Yes, she's right. We're happy to have you here." Bella smiled at herself for jumping the hurdle of finding speech in an uncomfortable situation. "Thanks for helping me up. I swear, there are days when I have two left feet, even in sneakers like I have on now."

"Looks like you're fine," he said.

Bella could fall and die on those words. Most of all, she would give the man the world from the way his golden-brown eyes seared into her. There was some sense of recognition in them. She would have remembered ever meeting him before, so she had to assume that he may seen something about her that he liked; she certainly hoped so. She could only hope her reaction wasn't visible to the naked eye. *Naked.* She needed to stop. The man had her thinking of all kinds of things that involved need and them being naked. She shook it off and put her professional face on.

"You said Kenneth, right?" she asked, finally discovering her brain again.

"Yes."

The drawl of his voice slammed into her like a hot, sexy punch to her gut and she loved it.

"Then I'm Bella and not Ms. Hardwick. This is Desiree, my best friend."

Before she could explain who she was, Desiree slid her own hand out for Kenneth to shake.

"I'm also her hair stylist," she said.

"You always look amazing and now I see that you made a good choice in who works on you. Your hair looks nice."

"Thank you."

Bella started walking and engaged him so that he would walk with her.

"I'm going to check on Dana to be sure she's ready to touch up your makeup as soon as you're ready. It was nice to meet you Kenneth," Desiree said and walked away.

Being alone with him, Bella wanted to be nervous but when she looked up into his smiling face, she realized she had never felt more comfortable in the presence of any man than what she was feeling right now.

"What do you think of the set so far? Will my body double be safe in that scene with the car blowing up?" Bella asked him.

"Yes. We've checked and rechecked and she will be fine. The other scenes that are notable are the ones with you in them and we're checking the safety of the gear for that. One involves a fire engine exploding. There are lots of controlled explosives."

"I'm used to it. Most of my movies have a lot of action scenes like that," she said.

As they walked, Bella noticed everything about him from his height of at least six-five or close to that and the comfort in his long strides.

"I enjoy your movies and so does my daughter. You're her favorite actress," he said.

"How old is your daughter?"

"She's nine going on nineteen. She wants to one day direct movies in Hollywood. She's begging to come to the set and see all of this and to meet you."

"Bring her! I would love to meet a future director. Who knows, there may come a day when she may be directing a movie I'm in. Wouldn't that be a hoot?" she asked gleefully.

"I wouldn't want to intrude on your time or this opportunity I've been given, being here providing my insight."

"Nonsense. If she wants to one day be a director, this set could be that one point in time that will guide her future career. I'm all about empowering young girls to do what they want in life, especially when it comes to being behind the camera and not just in front of it. Would your wife like to visit the set as well?"

She was reaching and she knew it. She's never been a forward kind of woman but this brother was too good looking to not get all in his business. She wanted and needed to know, not that it would lead to anything. When he laughed and smiled down at her, he was letting her know that she was digging.

"There's no wife; only an ex-wife who has remarried and had a baby with her husband, who makes her very happy."

"You have a good relationship with her?" Bella asked.

"Yes. We were once in love and married. I'll forever have a good relationship with her no matter what. We share a wonderful daughter. It was an equitable divorce and we're still friends. I was even invited to her wedding. How is that for proving divorces don't have to be full of contention."

"That's amazing and I love it. You should check with security and get your daughter access. When you do, make sure you stop her by my trailer for a little girl chat about the industry. How's that?" she asked.

"Are you sure? You don't mind? Willow will blow a fuse with so much excitement."

"I don't mind at all. In fact, I look forward to it. I'll even have a few autographed items for her. She'll have a good time checking everything out."

"That's amazing. I really appreciate it. We watched one of your movies recently, *The Jinx Who Was King*. It's one of our favorites. Let me just say right now that my daughter is a walking library when it comes to action and adventure movies. She gets that from watching movies like that with me since she was a baby. She knows all of your movies word for word."

"A true fan. I love it. Are you a true fan as well?"

"I will be an even bigger fan if I can get some autographed gifts as well. She's not the only fan in this family."

"You got it. Anything for the man who saved me from falling on my face."

"Now, Bella! You're up," her production assistant yelled in her direction when she rounded the corner to where everyone was waiting on her.

"That's my cue that I need to get going. It was nice to meet you, Kenneth. I look forward to seeing you again."

"That feeling is mutual."

As she walked off ahead of him rushing to get to the set, Bella couldn't resist the temptation of looking back to see if he was still watching her. When she turned her head slightly to the right, she saw that he was and that made her day.

"Santa, can I have that man under my tree on Christmas morning? Perhaps many mornings after that? I promise I won't ask for anything else; just that genuinely kind-hearted man. Why can't I ever find a man like that and ride off into the sunset," she said to herself.

When no answer came, she knew why. It was because of all the frogs she continued to kiss while not allowing herself to be open and free for her true prince.

4

Kenneth walked into his house, exhausted after a long day of being on the movie set. He was expecting to see Willow up and running to greet him at the door, but that didn't happen. Instead, he found his best friend in the whole world, Gabriella Reed, on a ladder in his family room attempting to decorate the top of the tree.

"Gabby, what are you doing? You should not be that high on a ladder!" he said, racing over to brace the ladder to keep her from falling.

"What? Oh, please. I've been on ladders this high before. Stop acting all *he-manish* and stuff. I'm good," she said descending the metal steps.

Kenneth watched her step back to take a look at her work on the silver, red and green decorations.

"Looks good. Where's Willow?" he asked.

"In bed. Can you believe it? It's only nine in the evening. Usually, she's asking to stay up to wait for the Jimmy Fallon show. When you called from the set to tell her that tomorrow was the day that she could go with you after waiting three days, she was full of energy. She was like a movie star getting ready for her first starring role."

With Willow in bed, Kenneth went to his beverage center off of the side of the kitchen and grabbed a beer. He never drank when she was awake, but enjoyed indulging at the end of a busy day like today.

He spent the day checking electrical equipment and building flooring for any safety concerns. While on a break, one of the production assistants gave him the news that he was cleared to bring Willow by the set. With her being home schooled, he didn't have a problem with taking her away from her school work for one day in the middle of the week.

"What did she do?" he asked going back into the family room in search of the remote to the seventy-five-inch television on the wall above the fireplace.

"First, she said she wanted dinner early, which I made. She took her bath early, had me fix her hair in a bun and let me tell you, that was no easy fete with all that hair she has, even with it in long braids. I swear it grows longer each time I see her. Soon, she'll be sitting on it. I got it done though."

"I know. Her mother thought about cutting it, but Willow said no and I told Carrie to leave it alone. She loves her long hair. It's usually in braids, especially when she comes here. If it's not, either my sister or the babysitter does it for me."

"She told me that. She even laid out the perfect outfit across the bed in the guest bedroom. I must say, my goddaughter has amazing fashion-sense. It's a good thing I wasn't planning to stay the night in the guest room. I would have to sleep in a corner of the bed to not ruin her outfit. She said she didn't want it to get wrinkled. I even ironed everything for her. Do people even iron clothes anymore?" she kidded.

"I do and that's not for me, it's for her. She loves fashion and it must be neat and perfect at all times, which means, me ironing. I don't let her do it yet."

"I knew it wasn't for you. Remember, I've seen you at your worst and that's when you didn't even consider an iron!"

"You got jokes I see. The tree is looking good. You know I appreciate you helping finish it up and watching Willow today. How was her school work?"

"She did fine. She's still very much an "A" student. Even virtually, she is never distracted from her school work. I kept checking and each time, she was fully focused on her instructor."

"That's because she has plans of going to film school one day and I told her she has to start getting and keeping good grades now."

"True, true. What does she want Santa to bring her for Christmas this year? I need ideas. Between you and Carrie, y'all get her everything, leaving nothing for me and Ray to get for holidays and birthdays. I want to get her something good."

"I knew you were going to say that and I kept the best just for you. Even Carrie isn't going to touch it."

"Okay, clue me in."

"She wants a bike and even picked it out. She also wants rollerblades and a new pair of ice skates. You pick which one you want to get and the rest will go back on the list for Carrie and I to split."

"Let me get all of those. You know I love spoiling her. Who knows if I'll ever have kids of my own? If not, I have this little girl and she's my everything; you know that."

Kenneth knew that there was never a doubt that Gabby would be the godmother to any and every child he had. He didn't have a better friend in the world. Without a doubt, Willow loved her with everything in her.

"Hey, I'm not one to argue. Her list wasn't long this year, but it's a little pricey. She's also getting a cellphone for the first time. Carrie and I talked about it and Willow has been asking for one all year."

Gabby looked at him in that cop kind of way. Being a detective, she was all about being safe, especially when it came to kids and cell phones.

"As the cop in this crew, make sure you let me have a sit-down with her about cellphone safety just like I did about computer safety. There are so many crazies out there."

"Carrie already told me to ask you about doing that. We could do it, but you being a cop, you know Willow looks up to you and heeds your advice, not from a mom and dad perspective."

"You know I got you covered. Now, what is Santa bringing you this year?" Gabby asked.

Kenneth looked over at the woman who has been his right arm since they were kids, and grumbled. She was always trying to rope him into some gift she could get him. This year wouldn't be different from any others. He still had nothing to offer.

"Did I tell you what Willow thinks should be under the tree for me this year?" he asked, changing the subject.

"A woman?"

He sucked his teeth at her. She knew them too well.

"No just any woman, but Bella Hardwick."

"What? Gorgeous action actress Bella Hardwick? Are you serious? Wait, let me get something to eat so that I can get comfortable while you tell me how this came about. You want a sandwich while I'm making myself one?"

"Yeah. One piled high with ham and Swiss would be great if you don't mind."

"Not at all. Hold the conversation until I return. I don't want to miss anything.

Kenneth nodded and searched through television channels to put the news on and quickly hit the mute button. He preferred reading it in closed-caption as he thought about Bella. Gabby had asked if he was serious and little did she know, he was more serious than he'd ever been. Not only had Willow put the idea in the air, he'd been thinking about it even more since meeting Bella in person.

After working around her for the past three days, he was actually thinking about asking her out for coffee or perhaps dinner. They seemed to seek each other out whenever they had a break. Others began noticing as well. When she wasn't on set, she was off to the side engaged in conversation with him. He found himself excited about their chats. Even Desiree would leave them together as she mysteriously found something else to do besides sit with them. He had learned a lot about Bella.

She had been born and raised in Raleigh, North Carolina, where her parents still lived, but were currently on a holiday vacation, courtesy of her. She had a brother she loved very much who had kids she adored. She mentioned that she had recently broken up with her philandering boyfriend, Brandon West, Hollywood heartthrob and well-known playboy. Like everyone else, he had a front row seat to how Brandon messed over her and she didn't deserve that. She needed a good man; a better man; the best man. Is that him? He didn't know. He was reaching, but his desire for her grew with each interaction. He loved watching her in action.

He told her all about Willow and his life as a fireman. She loved hearing about some of the real fires he'd fought. She said she watched him on the controlled fire sets and how much she loved watching him work. She was happy they always used actual firemen on their movie sets. They were the best to have when it came to real safety.

He found himself mesmerized, not just by her beauty, but by how knowledgeable she was on politics, other movies, not just her own and finance, topics that interested him also. She told him that before her career took off as an actress, she was in college studying financial management, something she was hoping to get back to one day. She only had two years to go before completing her degree. He encouraged her to never forget to go back to it if that's what she wanted. Even though he had an undergraduate and graduate degree in Health Administration, his life's passion had always been to save lives and so he became a fireman. He was being groomed to take over as chief, but for now, he wanted to have his free time to spend with Willow during her most critical years. He would have time to dream chase later.

Asking Bella out had been on his tongue since day one. Three days in and he hadn't made any kind of move. Each time he thought about it, he wondered how inappropriate it would be for him to do so. Then he would get a vibe that she was feeling him too and may be waiting for him to ask, but he couldn't do it. She was used to superstars and million-dollar athletes. His biggest purchase was the five-hundred-thousand-dollar house he lived in with a thirty-year mortgage to pay for. She had boyfriends who could buy a house like his for cash and never care if they lived in it or not.

Bella was said to be worth over a hundred-million dollars. She was younger and way out of his league. Outside of all of the things that made them different, they had a lot in common.

For starters, like him, her favorite holiday was Christmas. They talked about loving the decorations, especially light extravaganzas the people loved to really dive into when it came to decoration their houses. He may ask if she's like to visit some neighborhoods he loved. Perhaps he would get around to that.

He loved seafood and she shared, before he did, that her favorite foods were all seafood. He was obsessed about working out and she shared that she had to make time every day to get her workout in and she didn't care what time of day that was. He could relate. He'd turned an entire room on the lower level of his house into a home gym. Though she was an action actress, she had a love for sci-fi movies like him and they had fun diving into talking about the best and worst of those movies they could think of.

Earlier in the day, they ate lunch together where he told her that he finally got permission to bring Willow on the set. Bella was more excited than he was. He was happy that he could make her smile and give Willow a day she'll never forget. He thought about how Gabby said that he and Carrie gave Willow everything. He didn't think they gave her everything, but most of all, they gave her love and a hope for a future filled with her dreams from now and later in life. Gabby was just as guilty at spoiling Willow as he and Carrie were.

He and Gabby had been friends since elementary school and best friends since high school. They had never, ever dated and the idea of it sickened them both when people brought up how close they were growing up. What they didn't know is that he and Gabby saw each other as brother and sister.

One day some kids were picking on Gabby on the school bus ride home when they were in the fifth grade. She didn't have anyone protecting her. When one of the boys took out some scissors and passed them around to another boy who was going to secretly cut Gabby's hair, Kenneth stood up and beat the boy up on the bus. His parents first gave him a tongue lashing he would never forget about keeping his hands to himself and then they walked with him over to Gabby's house to make sure she was okay. The next day, as he got back on the school bus, where he wasn't banned from being on after the bus driver told what he saw, his father accompanied him. He thought his father was going to make him apologize to that brat kid, Dennis. Instead, his father reminded him, publicly, that he should always be the knight in shining armor to protect a girl and if he ever sees a girl being bullied again, he should look forward to being suspended, but he would receive no punishment at home. He would get in trouble at home if his father found out he didn't protect a girl in need. When he looked toward Dennis, he told him to feel free to have his father call him if there is a need for a conversation but he should expect that his son will give him another beating if the need arose.

That was the first day he saw his father as a real hero. It was also the day that he and Gabby became friends and stayed that way. Their friendship didn't need to be explained. Gabby was still best friends with him and Carrie and she didn't take sides in the divorce.

Gabby had been married once, herself, until the man she married discovered that she couldn't carry her own children due to a medical condition. He left her and found another woman that could. She was currently dating a guy, Ray, a firefighter who didn't care about that and told her that one day, she would adopt a baby that would be her own. He only hoped that their relationship would get them to that day together.

He looked up when she entered the room and handed him a plate with a well-stacked sandwich with chips on the side.

"You make the best sandwiches!" he said just before taking a man-size bite out of it.

"Hurry up and chew that and tell me about Bella. I want to hear everything. Maybe Santa will put her under your tree this year. I know you and Carrie didn't work out and Kim, well, you know I didn't like her because she did nothing but complain about the time you spent at the fire house saving lives. Who couldn't appreciate a man who has made it his life's journey to fight fires? Besides, my man fights fires everyday too, so conversations with Kim started to get right tricky."

"True. Well, Bella has no problem with firefighters. She also can't wait to meet Willow tomorrow. I told her how Willow wants to direct movies and she jumped right on the bus offering to show Willow around and to introduce her to the team. She's going to give her some free autographed stuff and check this out – I haven't told this to Willow yet. She's going to get the chance to play the role of a child at play in the park in the movie that Bella is shooting. Her role will call for her to wave at Bella during the scene."

"What! That's amazing! She's going to be so stoked. Maybe she'll be an actress and get in front of the camera instead of behind it. Did you tell Carrie about it?" she asked.

"I called her right away to be sure she was good with it. Her only complaint was that she's out of town and wouldn't get to meet Bella and see Willow in action on set. I told her I would take pictures to send her but that she couldn't share them with anyone. I'm allowed to take five pictures for my own personal use, but not for any public use or social media until after the movie comes out."

"You are about to become Willow's favorite person in the world for the rest of her life. You know that, right?"

"I'm her hero!"

"Okay, hero. I've one more hour before I have to get out of here and pick up Ray. He's got the next two days off and I'm going to hold him hostage at home. You know, introducing me to Ray has always been one of your greatest gifts to me. I want you to know that after I hear about Bella and I find that she would be perfect for you, I'm going to push you in that direction. As happy as you've made me by telling me that you thought he and I would be a great couple, I want the same for you."

"You sound like Willow. You do know who Bella is, right? She's a world-star actress worth millions. She has men clawing for her attention every day. I'm not in her league, though it's scary to think that we have so much in common, but are so far apart."

"Nonsense. Her being a star and rich doesn't mean she's out of reach or out of your league. Do you remember one Christmas when we were kids in high school and I wanted Damian, the star of the football team to ask me out to the winter dance and I thought I was far from the kind of girl he would want on his arm? You told me to never think of myself as out of reach of anything or anyone; that he would be lucky to have my interest. You were right and he did ask me to the dance. He was a terrible date, but I developed so much confidence after that. You may think Bella couldn't possibly be interested in you, but I know different. I'm your best friend and I may be a little biased, but her life would be greatly enhanced if she took notice of what a true gem you would be. You would definitely be better than her current selection of a man."

Kenneth chuckled. He had been thinking the same thing.

"I hear you and thanks for always being in my court."

"Cool, cool – so now, tell me all about Bella and don't leave anything out about your mutual attraction because I already know it to be true. I know you're smitten with her. When you called me yesterday to tell me you met her and you needed me to watch Willow while I was off today, I could hear it in your voice."

"She's a remarkable woman and I can't stop thinking about her. From the minute she fell into my arms, not in the way you think though, she's been on my mind."

"Fool, start from the beginning with the falling in your arms part. That's got to be romantic because you're looking all star-struck and stuff. Tell it to me slow, but then fast enough that I get it all before my hour is up. I've got food, snacks and a cold beer. I'm comfortable, so hit me with the details!"

Kenneth chortled, took another big bite of his sandwich and settled in to tell a story.

"Okay. She was coming out of her trailer on my first day there, and she tripped down the steps. I grabbed her before she ended up face first in the dirt, hence, the part about her falling into my arms."

"This is going to be good!" Gabby said.

It was good, Kenneth thought. Gabby had no idea how good the past three days have been for him.

5

"How do I look?"

Bella was a ball of nerves. Being this excited over a man was not her usual game of play, but there was something about Kenneth. Just his presence had her more excited than she'd ever been with any man, even Brandon, who she had been at her most vulnerable with. There was something about Kenneth that had her up early, in her trailer before the sun came up, even though, the scenes she was shooting wouldn't occur until later in the day. She had to see Kenneth and she wanted him to see her. Today was the day that he was bringing his daughter with him. She could use that as an excuse for being up and here earlier than she was known to be when she had late shoots. She looked at Desiree, who showed up to do her hair, and Dana, her makeup artist who slayed the job of making up her face every day. When they yawned together, she tried to stifle a laugh, but couldn't.

"I'm not speaking to you right now," Dana said, sitting on the pink chaise lounge with her legs crossed, eyes barely open.

"Child, please. Being up this early is not new for you," Bella goaded. She loved using her power of persuasion to draw her friends into her plans. She needed them and she had no problem letting them know how much.

"It is when I'm supposed to be able to sleep until ten. You aren't schedule to be on set until noon. You don't even have a dry-run scheduled, yet I get this middle of the night text that asks, no, begs me to be here at five in the morning. I had a late night in anticipation of sleeping in," Dana complained.

"Oh, Dana, lighten up. Can't you see that there is something different about Bella today? Look closely at our friend. Being here this early has nothing to do with this movie. This, my dear, is about a man!" Desiree chimed in.

Bella waved her off.

"You think you know everything," she protested.

Desiree walked over to Bella whose face Dana had already worked on and now it was time for hair."

"I know that I'm doing your hair, per your request, as if you're going out on a date. That means, the little to no makeup that Dana put on you this morning and the sexy way you want me to do your hair means there is a man involved. You don't have to deny it. We're your girls and we're here for it all!"

Bella looked up at Desiree and then over at Dana. She did try to hide what was going on with her this morning, but her face wouldn't allow her to continue that charade. She smiled and gave them a thumbs up.

"I love it!" Dana exclaimed happily.

"I knew it. She's never been like this with any other man, not even that heathen, Brandon."

Desiree threw up her hands in defense knowing Bella was about to fuss at her.

"I second that!" Dana declared.

"And before you jump all over me, where is the elusive boyfriend? Still in Paris or perhaps he snuck off to another location without telling you? What would he think right now about your behavior over the hunky fireman?" she added.

Bella brushed off the idea that she cared what Brandon was doing or who he was doing. Since the moment she met Kenneth, he was the only man she thought about constantly. He's the first man to ever replace all thoughts of Brandon. That's saying a lot considering she was usually distracted with all of Brandon's shenanigans, which she often read about in the latest gossip blog. He would then follow up any salacious stories about him by a phone call full of apologies and promises to never mess around on her again.

"Brandon can think whatever he likes. We're not together as a couple anymore."

"Really? I thought you were celebrating Christmas

with him in Paris this year. That's what you told me after he gave you the brushoff for Thanksgiving. I mean, who invites someone for Thanksgiving with his family and he doesn't show up? I can't imagine how uncomfortable that had to be for you sitting around the table with his entire family without him," Desiree alluded.

Bella sighed through the memory of giving up Thanksgiving with her own family this year to spend it with Brandon and his family. Their relationship had been rocky for quite some time. She hadn't seen him since Labor Day weekend in Miami where they faked through a weekend event together, specifically for all of the cameras flashing around them. Her smile had been as fake as his, knowing that nothing about them being together was real anymore.

She had hoped he would stop cheating on her and realize what they could have together as the newest Hollywood power couple. She was bothered that he enjoyed coupling with everyone else except her. How she allowed herself to get caught up in someone else's life and not get out of it what she put in, she didn't know.

"At one point, I really loved Brandon. For a while now, it has turned into some kind of obsession to turn him into the man I want him to be. I thought Labor Day weekend would be the turnaround point and we would work on our relationship, but that didn't happen. It ended as fake as it had started. Then the Thanksgiving invitation came and I thought, okay, maybe he's ready. When I got to his parent's chalet in Spain and he wasn't there, I figured his flight had been delayed. The fact that his family knew he wasn't coming and were surprised that I was there was one of the most embarrassing moments of my life. They took pity and let me stay. The entire dinner was awkward. I was supposed to stay three days, but the next morning, I took a flight back here to Maryland. I keep having these moments were I continually fall for his many excuses."

"You seem to have a lot of those when it comes to him. Have you really broken free of his grip? Dana and I love you like sisters and we're tired of how Brandon uses you for photo opportunities. Other than those times, have you had any time alone with him? When was the last time?" Desiree inquired.

Bella looked from Dana to Desiree, ashamed of what her admission was about to be.

"Christmas last year," she said.

"What? Oh, that's right because for Valentine's Day this year, he was shooting a movie and you went to surprise him on set."

Bella prayed Desiree wouldn't offer up the obvious elephant in the room; what truly happened on that day made for lovers. It was a day that should have been made for her and Brandon, but things didn't quite turn out that way.

"Was that when...?" Dana's question trailed off.

Bella sighed. If she could be honest with anyone, it

was with her two best friends.

"Yes. That was when I found him with those two groupies in his hotel room."

"Did that hotel manager get fired for giving you the cardkey to his room? I know she knew who you were and that you and Brandon were supposedly a couple, but that caused a major stink. The media had a field day with that," Dana asked.

"The hotel wanted to fire her, but I intervened and she was able to keep her job. She is one of the nicest women I have ever met. She wanted me to know what he'd been doing behind my back. She told me she knew it was wrong, but she couldn't stand to see him treat me like I was nothing."

"Brandon is a good looking brother and doesn't have to do much convincing. He is a snake, though, and I'm glad to see you're finally moving on from him."

"I think I was more in love with what he and I could build together. It's hard dating in my line of work. I can't think that any man would want me for me and not just because I'm famous," Bella confided.

"Famous, rich and beautiful is what you are. What about Kenneth then? He's not rich and famous and yet here we are, in your trailer at the butt-crack of dawn working on your makeup and hair," Desiree offered.

Bella wasn't even sure she knew. All she could muster up as an explanation was the truth and even that blew her away because it was out of character for her to fall for anyone as fast as she'd fallen for Kenneth.

If there was such a thing as love at first sight, she had experienced it and it wouldn't shake her free.

She turned to the mirror to check her hair and then turned back to face them.

"Do either of you believe in love at first sight?" she asked.

"Yes," both Dana and Desiree said at the same time.

Bella giggled like a school girl.

"Well, okay then. Take a few more minutes to decide if you need to," she quipped.

"No need. Why do you ask?" Dana said.

"I can't really explain it, but my eyes settled on Kenneth and in my head, I saw us cuddled up, relaxing, having the kind of one-on-one moments I have always dreamed about. That's not easy to have when it comes to me. When he shook my hand, a sudden rush of heat fused through me, straight to my heart and then my head. I saw him and me married with babies running around. I was stupid happy like never before. The visual went away when he let go of my hand. I saw it just as clear as I'm seeing the two of you. I know it sounds crazy, but I swear that happened. I saw a large Christmas tree with all the trimmings. I saw two little girls and one older all dressed up in fancy dresses for Easter and two little boys, spitting images of Kenneth decked out in little suits with short pants running around a big yard searching for Easter eggs. Kenneth and I were chasing behind them laughing and playing around."

She started to continue, but then saw huge smiles on Desiree and Dana's faces and wondered what they were thinking. Perhaps they thought she needed to have her head examined.

"Who are you and where is our friend? Girl! That's it! See what I'm saying is, you can have the life you've always wanted with the right man," Dana exclaimed.

"Yes! That's what I'm talking about. Dream it, see it, believe in it!" Desiree claimed.

Bella was surprised. Those were not the responses she expected.

"You don't think I'm out of my mind with all that?" Bella asked.

"Dana and I have had a front seat to everything Brandon has taken you through for the past couple of years and for what? I, personally, have hoped and prayed for someone not like Brandon, but more like the guys we grew up with, the ones in our families and close friends. I'm talking about the kind who appreciate a southern born girl like you who, yes, is living out her career dream and is at the top of her game but longs for something that this Hollywood lifestyle may not provide."

"I thought someone like Brandon was who I would need in order to not worry about being used and taken advantage of by a man who saw me and saw his way to a come up."

"You mean exactly what Brandon is doing? What

you saw with Kenneth is what we talked about as friends in school. Remember when we took that Cosmopolitan magazine survey about the perfect man? Yours didn't come out to be some Hollywood playboy. Your perfect man loved you from the inside of himself, while loving the inside of you; seeing your heart and appreciating that. Maybe that's who Kenneth is," Desiree explained.

"Do y'all remember when we made wishes back then? We wanted the same things that our own parents have. People take love and marriage for granted these days, but we didn't come from that kind of stock. Look at your parents, Bella. They are still very much in love after thirty-five years of marriage. My mom and dad have been married for thirty years and I swear, when I go home to visit, I can hear their bed squeaking night after night. I've learned to get a hotel room," Dana snickered.

"I learned a long time ago to stop sleeping under the same roof as my parents with all of their amorous activities," Bella joked.

"Desiree's mom and dad have been married almost fifty-years with eight children and we all know they have the perfect love. Desiree and her wife survive her schedule of traveling around with you and other celebrities doing hair all over the world, but when she gets home, there are no issues. They love harder when they get their time together. We have always been around forever and you deserve that," Dana explained.

"Before meeting Kenneth, I'm not sure I knew what I wanted at this time in my life, but I saw it. I spent some time talking to him the past few days on my breaks and the one word that comes to mind when I'm with him is, *home*. He makes me think of what home is supposed to be. It's that feeling of being comfy and cozy, loving and enjoying every moment together. Holidays would be special times together and family would always be the priority. I feel all gooey and silly with him and it feels good. He's easy to talk to and when he smiles, my heart skips several beats."

Bella had never put herself out in the open like she was doing. Something has come over her and Kenneth is the cause. She wanted to know much more about him, spend more time with him and never lose the feelings he brings out in her.

"You were always on edge with Brandon – all uptight wondering what skeleton was going to rear its ugly head. It's Christmas; a time for dreams to come true. See, now I'm feeling much better about being here this early to help you get ready for this dream man. You know you don't need any makeup or to have your hair done. You're naturally beautiful, so why are we really here?" Desiree asked.

Her friends knew her so well. Bella smiled to herself.

"I only needed your support. There is something different about today. I'm going to meet his daughter. She wants to one day direct and produce her own movies and I want to make a good impression."

"So? You don't need us for that. Kids love you," Desiree offered.

"No, kids love the characters I play in my action and sci-fi movies. I really like Kenneth and what if his daughter doesn't like me? Supposed she sees me as a snob or something?" Bella asked, more nervous now than when she first arrived.

When her friends laughed uncontrollably, she tapped her foot in frustration.

"I'm sorry. We're not laughing at you, but at what you said. You are the one actress furthest from being a snob. That's what this is about? A little girl? You want to win her over? You really like him this much?" Desiree asked.

"I swear I'm not crazy, but yes. A handshake and a few conversations with the most incredible man in the world and yeah, I like him that much. I've got some stuff I want to autograph for her and a few other gifts. I need you to tell me I didn't go overboard."

Before they could continue, there was a knock on her trailer door and all three of them jumped to attention. When Dana stood to open the door, Bella stopped her.

"She got this!" Desiree exclaimed.

Gathering her nerves, she walked over and opened the door and on the other side stood Kenneth with his daughter, a shorter, female version of him.

"Hello," she said. Bella didn't even recognize her

own voice. When did she become so soft-spoken when she had just been loud and boisterous with her friends? She knew it was all a part of the softer side that Kenneth brings out in her and she loved it.

"Hi there. You look amazing any time of day, huh? Even this early? Are we too early? If so, we can come back," Kenneth said, smiling at her.

Bella's heart skipped at beat hearing the sexy, baritone-filled words.

"Thank you and no, you're not at all too early. You're right on time. Who might this be?" she asked, looking to the little girl who waved so vigorously that Bella thought her hand may fly off.

"I'm Willow and this is my dad," she said pointing to him.

"She knows who I am," Kenneth said.

"Oh, that's right. You sure are pretty, isn't she daddy? I told you she would be beautiful and not just on the movie screen. My dad lets me watch all of your movies. They are my favorites."

"Thank you. I'm glad you like them. That is so nice coming from a beauty such as yourself. Well, I'm Bella," she said, offering her hand to Willow to shake.

"Miss Bella," Kenneth corrected.

"Sorry about that. I'm so used to introducing myself to adults. Can I call you Willow?" she asked as they continued shaking hands.

"Yes, Miss Bella. It's a pleasure to meet you."

"I feel the same way. Why don't you and your father

come inside out of the cold."

Once inside with the door closed, Bella did introductions all around. With a quickness, Desiree and Dana suddenly remembered they had something else to do and left. She turned around to see Kenneth's big smile and, he was holding up a bag.

"I brought breakfast. Remember yesterday when I said a deli in my area had the best bagel breakfast sandwiches? I bought one for each of us along with hash browns, chocolate milk as well as coffee," he said.

"I asked my dad to get you a chocolate milk too just in case you wanted to try it. The bagels are really good with it," Willow said gleefully.

Bella moved about the trailer moving things around to make them more comfortable in their space. Any reservations she thought she would have meeting Kenneth's daughter flew out of the window.

"She did and I have coffee just in case chocolate milk isn't your thing. I hope this is okay. I didn't know what type of morning you were having."

When Kenneth spoke to her, she felt his words in her heart. He spoke to her in a loving way that had her feeling like they could have more. She sure hoped so.

He showed up in a different leather jacket, this one black which went well with is all black attire of a black turtleneck, black denims and on his feet, black Timberland boots. The black Fedora hat he now held in his hand that was on his head topped off his alluring attire.

For her own look for now, she chose a purple sweat suit with a white tank top underneath, with a pair of purple UGG boots. Realizing she was standing still, not talking but staring Kenneth down, she blushed and finally found her words again.

"Actually, my morning is pretty slow and I haven't had breakfast. I'm starving. I'll take a bagel sandwich and one chocolate milk. If Willow says they go great together, I believe her," she bellowed.

"Do you have a microwave to heat this up?" Kenneth asked.

"I do and while you do that, I'll get us some plates and stuff. My trailer is pretty stocked. So, Willow, I heard you want to be a producer and director one day," Bella said moving about the extra-long, extra-wide trailer that included a small bedroom in the back as well as a kitchen with a four-seat dinette. The front of her trailer was made for her to get ready for her time on set and when she wasn't she had a place that was as cozy as a hotel suite.

"Yes, and I also want to write. I do that all the time now. Daddy loves my stories."

"That's amazing! Your stories must be good. If you ever want another set of eyes on any of your stories, I am available to read them at any time."

"Really? Daddy, did you hear that? Is it okay? Can I share one of my stories with Miss Bella?" Willow asked.

"Of course, you can. I think she could give you

some good advice."

Bella was about to chime in when the phone on Kenneth's hip vibrated. He smiled at her and read the text message.

"Looks like they need me for a check for an early morning shoot. I guess they saw me arrive. I thought we'd have a little time to sit without interruption," Kenneth said.

Bella heard the sadness in his voice. He was overwhelming her with how much he seemed to enjoy being around her. She knew the feeling; it was mutual. She also knew and understood how important his role was to the movie.

"What are you going to do with Willow while you do that?" Bella asked.

"She wanted to see some of the set, so this would be a good time."

"Before she eats? That's fine if that's what you want, but she can hang out here with me, if you want. I have a lot of free time this morning. I can show her around. We can have some fun, again, if you're okay with that."

"Can I stay here, daddy? Please? Can I see the set later? I wanted to see Miss Bella acting," Willow pleaded.

"The two of you ganging up on me and I'm a lost cause. Yes, you can stay here. You have to mind Miss Bella and not get into anything. You know my rule about respect," he said.

"Yeah! Yes, I know. Thank you, daddy!"

"Before you leave, can I talk to you about something?" Bella asked Kenneth.

"Sure."

Bella walked back to the front of the trailer and turned to face Kenneth, leaning in close to talk so that Willow couldn't hear them just in case he didn't like her idea.

"I knew you were bringing Willow today and how you said she wants to one day be behind the cameras. I was able to secure her a small walk-on role of a child playing in the park behind me during one of my scenes. It won't require her to do anything other than play with the other children in the scene. I thought maybe she would enjoy that, if you think it's okay. There is some paperwork and several releases that need to be signed by you."

When he didn't respond, Bella thought that this was the moment when she'd finally messed up. She wondered how long it would take for her to say the wrong thing. Had she been too eager? Was she trying too hard? She suddenly felt the need to apologize for offering. Perhaps she had overstepped.

"I can't believe you would do that. Do you have any idea how crazy happy my kid is about to be? That is amazing! How could I ever thank you? She would be over the moon with excitement being able to tell her family and friends that she got to work on your set. Are you serious? You're sure it will be okay?" he asked.

Bella stood stunned. She thought she had done something wrong when she made him so happy that he actually picked her up and spun her around

"It's perfectly fine. When you go out, speak to my assistant, Shawna, who will point you in the direction of the director. I squared everything away and they just need you to look over all the paperwork. She's a minor, so there is lots of it. You're sure this is okay?" she asked.

"I'm about to show you how okay this is," Kenneth said. When he turned toward Willow, Bella beamed even brighter when she felt him slide his hand into hers as they walked toward the table here Willow was already eating and pouring two glasses of chocolate milk.

"This looks good," Bella said.

"Listen, Miss Bella has something she wants to share with you about your visit to the set today."

When he turned to her, Bella slipped into the chair across from Willow.

"Your dad mentioned you were coming today and I was able to get you a small part in the movie of a little girl playing with other kids during one of my scenes. You won't have any lines or anything. You'll just play and have a good time. I figured it would be great since you were going to be here all day. What do you think?"

Willow screamed with delight so loud that Bella laughed when Kenneth covered his ears. He must have known what was coming.

"Really? Can I daddy? Can I? I promise to do it

right. If you say yes, I promise to not get mad when I have to go to bed early and I mean for the rest of my life. I will load the dishwasher for the rest of the month. I'll be good all day. Can I? Please?"

Bella admired the exchange between them.

"How can I say no to that after all those promises. Yes, you can do it. I have to go talk to some people about it. Thank Miss Bella for making this happen."

"Thank you, Miss Bella. This is so exciting. My friends are going to be jealous."

"Eat your breakfast and I'll be back shortly. Don't you give Miss Bella any trouble."

"I promise, I won't. Thank you, daddy. Thank you, Miss Bella."

"Any time. The camera will love you. Let's eat breakfast and I can brief you on everything you'll need to do."

"Bella, are you sure?" Kenneth asked.

"I'm positive. Let me walk you out before they text you again," she said.

Once outside, she was the one who took his hand in hers this time, loving the feeling when they touch.

"Thank you for doing this for my daughter. She'll be talking about this for years to come. I need to call and check in with her mother, who I know will be okay with this."

"You will need her approval, which she can give vocally over the phone as well as email over."

More words were on the tip of her tongue, but she

couldn't seem to gather them in an intelligent way. The warmth she felt around him made her brain all fuzzy. She wanted to say so much, but couldn't figure out just what. Just when she was planning to just blurt out her words, he spoke up first.

"Listen, I hope this isn't inappropriate in any way and if so, just tell me and I'll never bring this up again. I was wondering if you would like to have lunch or dinner with me sometime. I know I'm not the typical guy you would probably say yes to, but I figured I would shoot my shot and take it on the chin if I'm being presumptuous. Am I overstepping?" he asked.

Bella beamed. He just did the most remarkable thing in the world. He took the pressure from her and put it on himself. He looked like he was about to take the words back when she squeezed his hand lightly, causing him to look down where they were connected before looking back up, giving her the perfect view of his dark as coal eyes, thick lashes and perfectly trimmed mustache and beard.

"No. I mean, no, you're not overstepping. I didn't mean no to dinner. Okay, let me try that again. Yes, to dinner or lunch. I was actually hoping we could. I came out to ask you if you wanted to hang with me some time off-set. I didn't want to do it in front of Willow. I would love to do anything, though it can be tricky," she said, pointing to her security who were on both ends of the outside of her trailer.

"I notice them every time I'm here. When I walked

up with Willow, I thought they were going to stop me, but instead, they waved me ahead."

"Oh, yeah, I told them you were coming by today," she replied.

"I don't mind them if you don't. I know they are here to protect you," Kenneth said.

"They'll help keep fans at bay. We may get swamped being out and about."

That was the part of her life that she didn't care for. She loved the fame, but there were times when she wished she could turn it off, especially if she was going to get the chance to be out on a date with Kenneth. She wanted to be selfish and have him all to herself without fans interrupting them.

"I see the large number of fans outside the filming area every day when I arrive. I assume it's always like that."

"It is. I do have a plan if you like a little cloak and dagger fun," she suggested.

"What did you have in mind?"

"Are we thinking lunch or dinner?" she asked.

"I was thinking a nice dinner where we could talk and get to know each other if that's okay with you. Interested?" he asked.

"Very."

"So am I" Kenneth responded.

Bella replied so fast, she shocked herself. They were connecting and she didn't want anything to get in the way.

She looked up at him and wanted to lay everything out on the line. This feeling she got with him was new for her and she wanted to chase it down with all power in her.

"You feel it too, don't you? I know what I've been feeling, but you feel it too. You're not just another man infatuated with the actress; it's me that you see, isn't it?" she asked.

She was going for it and didn't want to hold anything back.

Kenneth took her other hand in his and when he moved to the other side of her trailer away from prying eyes, her security moved with him until she put her hand up to them. The two bigger than life guys moved away, turned their backs to her, but still stayed within eye range. That gave them a little privacy.

The minute her head turned back to Kenneth, he was there. He was a whisper away from her lips.

"I see you and something about the way that you look at me shows that you see me too. It's not just what's on the surface; it's deeper than that. I thought that dinner could help us explore that a little further. I'm far from the Hollywood glamour, but I make great dinner company if you're up for that. I would like us to get to know much more about each other besides the mutual attraction, which I think we can agree is happening and has been happening since the minute we met. True?"

"Yes."

Bella wanted to say more, but she was focused on controlling her breathing. Her heart was practically beating through her chest for a way to escape being enclosed. How could she want and desire a man so much after only a few days and no date?

"Up for it?"

"I'm very up for that."

Bella allowed her eyes to travel from Kenneth's eyes to his lips which were still moving but for the life of her, she couldn't comprehend the words. His perfect lips were close enough for her to touch and kiss. She was trying to will his brain to do just that. Just a little closer, she thought and prayed his mind could read hers.

In the coldness of the morning, she could see the essence of each of his breaths escape his mouth just as hers was doing. They were equally fighting the obvious. She simply wanted a kiss. It didn't have to be a deep, passionate, unwavering kiss; just enough to get her through the day. She'd been thinking about what it would feel like to kiss him and being this close, she didn't want to walk away without finding out.

They breathed but didn't talk. They stared into each other's eyes. She let go of his hand and placed both of hers, palms flat, against his chest. She needed to brace herself against the magnetic pull to make the first move. Was he waiting on her? Before she could ask, Kenneth moved.

His head was moving closer, though she saw

hesitancy. Was he wondering if she would be receptive to a kiss? Boy, was she ever. Her eyes landed on his perfect lips and without them moving, they were calling to her. *Hello!*

Bella's brain was trying hard to send a signal that her answer was yes. To make her point clear, just in case Kenneth wasn't a mind reader, she moved a little closer to him, her sign that the coast was clear. The minute he read her silent agreement, she felt his lips on hers, soft at first and then demanding. She gave in and went with what she had been feeling from the start; this was perfection.

They moved together with precision, with ardor filled zest. His lips, against hers were soft, yet persistently aggressive. When she parted her lips a little, she delighted in his recognition of her need for more. The feverish kiss continued as her arms went up to grasp his shoulders while his hands enclosed her hips, pulling her snug against him. When his arms wrapped around her back, she moaned into the kiss, into his mouth just as his tongue slipped inside of her mouth and mated with hers. In this most private moment, he worshiped her mouth with a tenderness she'd never known before.

Bella's mind and body were about to explode as he quenched her starvation for the lascivious, lustful feelings that fed every electrifying need in every critical, sexy part of her body. She as on fire and never wanted to be doused.

When Kenneth pulled back a little, Bella moaned again. With the curve of his lips, he knew what he was doing to her. She saw his crave for her in his eyes the way she was feeling for him.

Kenneth once again took her lips vigorously feeding her need. This time, he licked across the seam of her lips from one end to the other, stopping in between to lay sweet kisses along the way. She felt like a mound of molten hot lava in his arms, ready to climb up his body.

In the next instant, his vibrating phone halted any more kissing. She was disappointed and could only hope that more of this was on the agenda for them at another time.

They parted.

"I think I'm being hailed again," Kenneth said.

Bella could see him trying hard to steady his breaths and his excessively beating heart. She was doing the same.

"Wow! I've never been kissed like that before," she admitted.

"Never?"

"Never. I felt that kiss all over me, not just on my lips."

Kenneth gazed at her and smiled.

"That's how a kiss is always supposed to feel. I better get going. My phone is not going to stop. I'll catch up with you and Willow as soon as I can."

"I've got her until you return. She'll be fine and safe

with me."

"With the security I see you have, she's in the safest place possible. They are watching over us while keeping a close eye on your trailer where she is. I like these guys already," he joked.

"Get used to it because they are like a second skin, most times."

"Oh yeah?" Kenneth smiled again.

"Not all the time though."

"That's a plus then. I'll see you soon?"

"No doubt."

With one quick kiss to her lips, she watched Kenneth jog off as she headed back into the trailer, caressing her own lips where his had just been. She'd never looked more forward to dinner with a man in her life. She danced a little as she went inside and joined Willow.

"Your food is getting cold," Willow said.

"I'll heat it up and then we can talk about how you want to write, produce and direct your own movies one day. We can also talk about what you'll be doing later. Is that okay?"

"Yes. I'm excited. Maybe I'll be an actress like you."

"I bet you can do anything in this world you set your mind too. Also, I have a few things for you for your first visit here."

"Can I see?" Willow bounced around in her seat as her eyes took in everything in the trailer, no doubt, Bella assumed, looking for what may be for her out in plain sight.

"Let's finish eating first. We have a lot to do today before we reconnect with your dad later."

"Miss Bella? Do you like my dad?"

"Yes, I do."

No hesitation at all. After that kiss, she wanted the world to know how much she liked Kenneth, including his daughter.

"That's good because he likes you too."

Bella smiled and grabbed her food to heat it up. Her thoughts turned into how she hoped this Christmas was better than last year where she spent that day and night waiting on Brandon who had, instead, decided to spend his Christmas in Bali after wrapping up a movie. He decided to extend his time through the New Year, forgetting that they had made plans to spend some quiet time together. She knew that she needed to up her relationship expectations to get what she wanted out of being with someone. Now may be her time and she was excited about it.

Kenneth reminded her of how much she loved the holiday season. It was magical, anything could happen and wishes could come true.

6

"Dad, should you wear a tie? You're going on a date with Bella Hardwick; sorry, Miss Bella. I think you need a tie. She might like that," Willow said.

Kenneth shook his head and smiled at Willow through the mirror, knowing she could see his face from her vantage point of sitting on the edge of his bed where she watched him get dressed for his date. As much as he wanted to see Bella a few days ago when he had originally asked her out, he came down to the reality that she wasn't someone who could just go out on a casual date on the town without causing mayhem once fans spotted and recognized her. She had to plan for every outing with her security team.

Since he didn't have to be on the set at all during the day, he and Willow spent the day doing a little extra Christmas shopping and he'd taken her ice skating down at the Inner Harbor. Their day out had been loads of fun and with her spending the night with her grandparents, he didn't have to worry about getting a sitter. He promised her that he would allow her to help him pick out his outfit.

They decided on black slacks and a black shirt, opened at the collar. In his opinion, he didn't need a tie; he actually hated the too-dressy look.

"I think I can pull this look off without a tie. What do you think?" he asked turning to her and letting her see all sides of him.

"You look great, dad. I think Miss Bella will love you in this."

"Thanks for telling me I needed to get a fresh haircut and shave today. It's a good thing Mr. Manny could fit me in."

"I like that barbershop in the city. Mr. Manny always has coloring books and other stuff for kids to keep them busy while their dad's get haircuts. He did a good job because you look fly daddy. Is Miss Bella going to be your girlfriend?" she asked.

Kenneth inwardly smiled at how nonchalantly Willow through those words into the atmosphere. She was so innocent. He wondered how long he'd be able to keep her that way. One day, he'll be helping her get dressed for her first day. He hoped that day was many, many, many years to come.

He liked being honest with her, though he watched the line he crossed in not sharing too much about adult things.

"I don't know. This is our first date."

"Are you going to a movie?"

"No, we're having dinner. I want to get to know her and you can't do that in a movie theater where people frown on talking," he jested.

"Oh, right. What are you going to eat?"

"I don't know yet. I'm going to Mr. Smitty's seafood restaurant. You know they have the best food and not just seafood."

"Can you bring me a crab cake home that I can eat when I come home tomorrow? Can I go with you to the movie set tomorrow?"

Kenneth realized he forgot to tell her that he'd gotten a call that the director liked her so much in the small scene she was in that he had a small speaking role for her that he wanted to shoot tomorrow. She would need to wear the same clothes she wore the first time. Luckily, he had washed clothes the night before and therefore, the outfit was ready

"Yes, I will bring you a crab cake and yes, you can come with me tomorrow. In fact, they need you to wear what you wore the last time. The director has a small speaking role for you. How exciting is that?" he asked.

Willow leaped up from the bed and was standing in front of him in so suddenly that he stepped back, not sure what her next move would be. He'd seen her excited before, but since the first day he took her to the set, she had been talking about it non-stop. That night when they finally made it back home, she had called her mother and he heard her talking for over an hour without pausing to give her mother a chance to say anything on the other end. He looked down at her as she danced around him with joy before stopping and staring him down.

"Stop! Really? I get to talk in the actual movie? Will I talk to Miss Bella? Will that make me a movie star?" she asked.

"No, you won't get to talk to her. From what I've been told, you get asked a few questions by a detective. If you remember, you were in the scene where Diamond, Miss Bella's character was meeting with an informant and just after she walks away, a man walked up and killed the informant. You and the other kids ran and scattered. The detective who shows up will ask you a few questions. It should be really easy for you to pick up. You are a natural. Are you sure you don't want to be an actress? You did everything so perfect. You're already a star," he encouraged.

Kenneth watched the idea float through Willow's head and she considered the idea.

"I think I might do both. I might be an actress who writes, produces and directs her own movies. What do you think about that?" she asked, giving him all kinds of poses as if she were in front of a photographer.

"Baby girl, I believe that you can do anything you set your heart on. The world is yours and yes, you can do it all."

"You always tell me that. You always say if I believe it, then I can achieve it; I can make it happen."

"That's why I have you saying that every single day. I never want you to forget that. You can have anything you want in this world if you dream and believe it."

"What about a wish?" she asked.

"A wish?"

"If I make a wish, will it really come true?"

"Have you ever made a wish before?"

"On my birthday and for Christmas. I always wish for Santa to bring me the best toys."

"Does he always come through?"

"Yes. I have a special wish for him, but I don't know if he can do it since it's not a toy."

Kenneth wondered what it was. He'd already gotten everything she wanted in the letter she wrote to Santa. Between him, her mother, her godmother and her grandparents, Willow got the things she asked for. They even got her extras for under the tree that they told her Santa wanted her to pick other children to give those to on Christmas day.

Every year, either him or her mother would take her to a local shelter after they have Christmas dinner. She could give toys to needy children to remind her that not every child lives the kind of life she has. She loved it and to them, it taught her humility and to have a heart for other people.

"Do you want to tell me? Perhaps it's something I can do to help."

"My wish is about you, so I can't tell you."

"Okay, then what about telling your mother? Did

you talk to her today?"

"I did this morning when you were still sleeping. Mommy said I shouldn't disturb you because you need the extra sleep when you're on vacation."

"You can always wake me up at any time. What kind of a wish are you making that's about me? You know I don't need anything for Christmas."

"Yes you do, dad."

"I do? What do I need?" he asked.

Kenneth had an idea of where the conversation was leading. They've had this conversation before.

"You need a girlfriend; someone to keep you company when I'm home with mommy. You're here all alone when I'm gone. Don't you want to be happy? Mommy used to be sad when it was just me and her and then she was happy again when she got a boyfriend. He's her husband now. She's happy all the time."

"I don't seem happy to you?"

"Sometimes."

"Willow, I'm happy all the time. I'm a little sad when you go home to mommy, but I get happy knowing that I'll get to see you again real soon. I can also drive to Pennsylvania anytime to see you, if you need me or if I just need a hug. I'm not unhappy. Trust me, having a girlfriend doesn't mean I will be happy."

"I know, but it could help, right? I told you about how my friends' moms all like you. I don't think you like any of them because you never went out on a date with any of them. Did you? Did you go out on a date with them?"

Kenneth laughed under his breath. He loved that he and Willow could talk about anything, but he noticed as she got older, a lot of their talks were about him. He didn't mind. He also didn't want her worrying about him.

"I've told you many times before that if there is a woman who is supposed to be my girlfriend, she will be. It's not your job to find me one."

"I know. It's just a wish. I know what I'll do," she said racing toward the bedroom door.

"Where are you going?" he asked as she headed out of his bedroom toward the steps.

"I'm going to make a wish on our tree. You said it was magical, right?"

He smiled never thinking his story of the lonely tree ending up in his truck would turn around to a story about wishes coming true.

"It's what I was told by Mr. William at the tree farm. He said the tree was magical. It sat all by itself. He said it was meant for me."

"See? I wonder if Santa will grant a wish made on the tree? I put my Christmas list in the mailbox and under our tree. I'm going to go have a talk with our tree while you find other shoes. I don't like those on your feet," she pointed.

Kenneth tried to respond, but all that came out was a hearty laugh as he looked down at the black shoes he'd slipped on his feet. She was right. He hated them too and walked into this closet to find another pair.

Willow was bluntly honest, which he liked. She wasn't afraid to say what was on her mind as long as she did it with respect. He also wondered if telling her that their Christmas tree was magical was a good idea. Supposed she did make a wish on their tree and it didn't come true? How would he explain how the magical tree really didn't have any magic?

He thought about her question of whether Bella would be his girlfriend. Should he even have a hope like that?

Last night, he'd been thinking about her and due to the late hour, he wasn't sure if calling her on the phone was a good idea. Who does that? What kind of common man decides to call a multi-million-dollar actress to ask her what she was doing? Instead, he sent her a text telling her that he would miss seeing her on the set the next day because he wasn't needed. He also let her know that he couldn't wait to see her at dinner. To his surprise, she didn't text him back, but instead, she called him. It was close to midnight by the time he had sent her that text, remembering that she had a late evening schedule on the movie set. He thought about their conversation as he sat on the bench at the foot of his bed and thought about how it went.

"Hello, beautiful. I didn't think you'd still be awake after your extremely long day. I was thinking about you and wanted you to know," he'd said.

"I was thinking about you too. I wanted to call

you, but I didn't want to disturb you this late. Are you still planning a fun day out with Willow in the morning?" she asked.

"I am. She went to bed early thinking the night would go by faster. We're going to start out early at her favorite diner for pancakes and fruit. I have a full day of fun planned."

"I love how you make sure she knows she's the priority in your life. My dad was like that with me when I was coming up. I wish I could do everyday things like eat at a diner or go shopping in a mall. I have to plan so much ahead of time and alerting mall security can be tricky. They're nice and cordial about it but I can tell that deep down, they wish that I would stay away. They are afraid that in the excitement of seeing a star, people would get trampled. It can get crazy. I long for simpler things in life."

"You mean there are issues with being a nationally known celebrity?"

"It's not all that people think it is. It's not as glamourous as the blogs make it appear to be. I would love to go get a milkshake or an ice cream sundae and sit right at the stand and eat it. I would love to go shopping without the owner actually closing the store for me to shop in peace. They do that in hopes that I'll spend a lot of money, which I do, to help make up for the lost sales with closing the store. I often feel disconnected with reality. Going, to say, a movie can be hectic if I try to go before the movie starts. In the

darkness of a theater, I can sometimes get away with it when people are focused on the movie. I have to sit way down front, but I can sometimes make that happen. I long for normalcy. Being me is not the best all the time. People will go above and beyond because of who I am when all I want is for them to treat me like anyone else."

"That's a tall order when it comes to the number one box-office actress."

"I know, but I can wish for it, right? Like on our date tomorrow night, I feel like I need to apologize upfront for all the interruptions we may get. When you told me where you wanted to take me, my team was able to reach out and get us a private space, but even then, I'm not comfortable with all they have to go through to accommodate me in their establishment. We compensate well for the inconvenience, but once, I want to be able to enjoy a meal and really pig out without cameras snapping everywhere. I've come across pictures of me putting food in my mouth and that becomes news on some blogs. Imagine that. It can get crazy."

"I wish I could make that happen for you," he'd said.

"I know, me too. It doesn't matter at this point. I'm just excited to see you on an actual date. I haven't thought anything else all day."

"Me, too, hence, the late-night text. I guess I'm a little anxious. I feel like a high school boy going out on

my first day with the cutest girl in school. I'm going to try and make the date as normal as possible. I was even thinking about taking you to my favorite Baltimore neighborhood to show you some spectacular Christmas lights. I know it may sound a little corny, but that's the kind of thing us regular guys do. Not impressive?" he asked.

"That's the most impressive idea I've heard from anyone. Now that you've mentioned it, you have to take me. I love, love Christmas time with all the decorations and lights. Usually, my parents are home for Christmas and they go all out with several trees with all the trimmings. My dad hires this company that comes out and decorates the whole house on the outside, front and back. There are lighted Santa's and reindeer on the lawn. It's quite a display."

"Then you would love my house. I add a little more to my decorations all the time until it's finally done in about a week or so. Willow thinks I have enough outside, but I don't know I'm thinking of somehow adding a Santa in a sleigh to the roof. It's still an idea I'm working on. We have this humungous tree that I've been told is magical. Willow and I finally finished decorating it last night and I must say, this is the best tree decorating we've ever done. I have more decorations up this year than any other year."

"I wish I could see it. That's the kind of stuff I miss; decorating the tree with my parents and brother. We did that every year when I was living at home as a

child. It was a big thing in my family."

"What do you do now?" he asked.

"The past few years, I've been wrapping up movies like this year and by the time the holiday rolls around, I end up paying someone to do it because all I want to do is rest."

"I hear you on that. You need more down time. You need more time to just relax and enjoy a moment of peace and quiet and if possible, a little Christmas decorating. I have a little more that needs to be done and if you're feeling up to it, maybe you'd like to come by my house one day and pitch in. We'll leave a few things out for you to add so that you can resolve the nostalgic moment you're having right now. I can hear it in your voice."

Kenneth meant every word of that. He could hear the sadness that can be the life of a celebrity which most people couldn't fathom. They seem to have it all, but most of the time, they just want to be able to have non-celebrity moments in public.

"I would love to do that. I hope you weren't just saying that to appease me. I really do want to see your tree. I look forward to seeing the lights tomorrow. What should I wear to be incognito?" Bella asked and laughed.

"For the festival of lights I'll take you to, you get to stay in the car. We'll ride from one neighborhood to another and take in the sights. The good part is no one can see inside of my darkened windows to know it's

you. Feel free to enjoy until your heart is content."

"Thank you for offering to do that. Thank you for being an amazing man."

"Anytime. I'll let you go since you have to be up early. Until tomorrow night?"

"Most definitely!" Bella cheered before hanging up.

Kenneth remembered tossing a little bit before finally able to turn his mind off from Bella's beauty and the thought that he would get time to relax with her off the movie set.

Now, here he was preparing to leave to drop Willow off so that he could pick Bella up. He had a few other things up his sleeve for her to enjoy what she saw as non-celebrity activities. At this point, he was in a trance, not just because she was the hottest, sexiest, most beautiful woman he'd ever met, but because she had a heart of gold. It was pure and that's something he loved the most about any woman he was interested in. He looked first to her heart and everything else was secondary.

**

Willow stood gazing at the tall Christmas tree, decorated in red and white balls with silver ribbon and bright white lights. She had picked out the color for this year. She wanted something bright and beautiful for the magical tree. In her red and white checkered pajamas, which she'd already put on for her overnight stay with her grandparents, she sat cross legged on the floor in front of the tree.

"I hear that you're a magical tree. If I make a wish, could you share it with Santa? It's not about toys or anything like that. It's not even something for me. It's all about my dad."

"See, my dad is the best dad in the whole entire world, and that's the truth. Everyone says so. Every day when he is working, he saves people's lives and houses from fires. He runs in to save children and doggies and cats and I worry about him. I guess I watch too many movies about firemen. My dad is careful, though. He doesn't want me to be sad so he makes sure he's safe all the time. I want to make a wish and hope that it can come true. This may sound weird but I'm hoping Santa can bring my dad a girlfriend for Christmas. I'm not talking about any ol' girlfriend. I'm talking about Miss Bella. She is so pretty and she likes my dad. My dad likes her a lot too. I can tell by the way he looks at her and talks about her. Tonight, he's going out on a date with her. Can you ask Santa to make the date a good one? Then, can he make her my dad's girlfriend forever? Maybe not forever because he should really marry her. I don't want to ask for that yet. I'll keep my wish small and just ask if he can make it so my dad has her as his girlfriend. He's a really good dad. Maybe he and Miss Bella will get married and have a baby like my mommy did when she got a boyfriend and got married. Anyway, I hear my dad coming, so I have to go now. That's my wish, oh magical tree. If you're really as magical as my dad says, then I hope you will share my wish with Santa right away. Christmas is coming up soon. Okay, thank you and see you later tree."

Willow stood, grabbed her overnight bag from the floor near the steps just as her father walked down.

"Are you ready?" he asked.

Willow looked back at the tree as she walked toward the garage door.

"I'm ready."

"Don't forget!" she whispered to the tree before closing the kitchen door behind her.

7

"Bella, we have a problem about your date tonight."

Hearing those words out of the mouth of one of her assistants made Bella exhale hard and loud. There was always something when she was preparing to have some time to herself.

"Micki, I swear if you tell me I have to cancel my date with Kenneth for any reason, no one is getting a Christmas bonus! I'm joking but seriously, what is the problem?"

Bella should have known something would go wrong. The minute she opened the door to her hotel suite to Michelle, who everyone called, Micki, she could see from the look on her face that something was wrong.

All day while on set, she had seamlessly gotten through every scene with no issues and even snuck in a text or two with Kenneth. She was now less than an hour from when her driver would drop her off for her dinner date and her assistant just threw gasoline on her moment while also holding the match in her hand, ready to drop it.

As Micki bit nervously on her bottom lip, Bella moved about her two-bedroom suite with plans to still go out. She needed this. Kenneth was a different kind of man than those she usually dated and she wanted this.

"It seems word got out that you would be at that restaurant tonight and already, a crowd has formed outside in anticipation of your arrival."

"What? How did that happen? No one knew about this but my team. There are six of you so who spilled?"

"I...I don't know. It wasn't me and I'm sure it wasn't Desiree or Dana," Micki explained.

"What about Felix? Shawna? Denim?" Bella asked.

"I don't think any of them would."

"Really? How is it that over the past year, more than a few of things I think are secrets within my team keep getting out?"

"Perhaps people are listening in on conversations and we're not as aggressive as we should be about making sure there are no ears around when we plan and talk."

Bella was frustrated. There was something or someone ripe on her team.

"Well, someone is leaking out my whereabouts. What happens now? I'm supposed to cancel my date because the restaurant, what, has a crowd outside?"

she asked.

"It's more than just a crowd. I was told there were several hundred people already gathered. Someone posted on social media that you would be having dinner there tonight. I'm sorry, Bella. I don't know how this happened. The reservation isn't even in your name."

"What now? Do I go out and Kenneth and I end up as the number one story tomorrow? I can't do that to him. You know how brutal they can be. I wanted a quiet night with him, not a rat race of us trying to duck and dodge the media. Are they still outside of the hotel?" she asked.

"I'm afraid so. I checked before I came to your room and I'm told paparazzi are waiting for you to come out."

"I know they camp out most of the time, but is it more or less than usual?" she asked.

"Many more tonight after word got out that you were going out to dinner. Everybody wants to know with whom."

"I hate this part of my life. Why can't I, for once, have a normal date? I'm not trying to sound ungrateful for all that my career has brought me but this guy is special. He's more special than any man I've ever met. Do I have to cancel now in order to protect him? I would do anything to keep him from being questioned and followed. I don't want him hounded the way they do me."

Before Micki, could answer, Bella heard her cell phone ring and knew that it was Kenneth. She had already created a special ring-tone just for him.

"Hey!" she said happily, trying to not seem bothered.

"Hey, yourself. How are you?" he asked.

"Excited about seeing you tonight. There may be a glitch," she said.

"Glitch? Oh, you mean about the crowd at the restaurant waiting for you to show up?" he acknowledged.

"They're waiting for us. I wanted peace and quiet for us. I should have known it would be too much to ask for."

"What do you want to do? Do you want to cancel and try another time? I understand if you do."

No, Bella's head screamed. Not seeing Kenneth after so much planning was not a part of her plans. She would offer her suite for them to have dinner, but there is no way to get him in without questions surrounding him. Not all hotel staff could be trusted to keep a secret.

"Bella, I have an idea," Micki said interrupting her call.

When she saw Micki with a big, wide grin on her face, she had to find out what she was thinking.

"Kenneth, hold on for a minute."

Putting the call on mute, she waited for Micki to explain.

"River Mays, your movie double on the set is still

here in the hotel. I just sent her a text to see if she was up for a little cloak and dagger mission tonight. She could go out as you and distract everyone. You and Kenneth could go someplace else. I can call and get you another reservation that no one would know about."

"That sounds good, but still, someone would recognize me and the crowd would eventually make a mad dash to the new location."

Bella turned back to her call with Kenneth.

"Everything alright?" he asked.

"My assistant and I are trying to find out how my double from the movie set could act as me so that I could slip out of here. I think that may work for a minute, but then the crowd will find out that it's not me and eventually end up at whatever other restaurant we decide to go to. I don't know what to do. I want to see you," she bemoaned.

"Look, I have an idea too. Let me know what you think about this. What if you still use your double and while she's being you, you can slip out from another exit of the hotel and into my truck. I told you about my dark windows, which I can get away with because I have a fire captain sticker on my window. Instead of going out to a restaurant, why don't we order all the food we want and we can go to my place for some real peace and quiet. No one will find you there. I know it may not be what we were planning, but I guarantee you there won't be anyone snooping around waiting for you."

"What about our drive through the Christmas villages you talked about? I want to see the lights."

"We can pick up our food and still do that. As much as you want to see me, I want to see you even more. I've been waiting all day for tonight."

"Me, too," Bella added.

She felt a renewed sense of excitement just thinking about it. She could have some quiet time with Kenneth and give her security team a night off. Could she do it?

"That sounds perfect. Do you think we can do it? If so, I'm all in."

"Good. Instead of restaurant attire, put something comfortable on. We can eat dinner, watch movies and talk in a relaxed atmosphere. Most of all, you can get a night out and away from prying eyes. I was already on my way to the restaurant. I can detour and come pick you up."

"Where would I go out?" she asked.

"I know everything about that hotel. I'll get that worked out once I call the manager directly. He knows me and will keep quiet. You work on your end. Make sure your double comes out with dark shades and maybe some kind of big hat. The minute she comes out of the front door, you will exit the door I tell you to come out of and we'll disappear into the night. Do you think your security will go along with this? I know how protective of you they are, and they should be."

"They won't be a problem and my double will be

happy to play along. She loves this kind of stuff."

"Sounds like a plan. I'll even cover her dinner if she wants to take our place at the restaurant. I'll call Smitty to see if he can have his son bring us some food. I'm thinking crab cakes, fried shrimp, lobster tails, vegetables and a few slices of cheesecake. How does that sound?" Kenneth asked.

"That sounds amazing. Can we stop somewhere to get me a milkshake? I've been thinking about that most of the day."

"Let's do that while we're driving through the Christmas lights. I know the perfect place to get some good ones with whipped cream and a cherry on top."

Bella was getting excited again.

"We can do this?" she asked.

"We are definitely doing this. Stay put and I'll call you back with details. I'm not letting anything keep me from see you tonight. I've been desiring those perfect lips of yours again. We kissed once and now, I feel like I can't breathe without another one."

Bella jumped up and down with more excitement than what Micki was used to. She could tell by the look on her face.

"I woke up thinking about our kiss this morning mad that I had to wait until tonight to get another one. Knowing you're as excited as I am makes it all the better. I'll take of things on my end and wait for your call."

"Be ready for me."

When the call disconnected, Bella turned to Micki. "It's all good. Kenneth is working things out. Go get River and tell her to put on something designer. Look in my wardrobe and find one of my staple floppy hats, big, dark sunglasses and a coat with a high collar to cover her face. I'm glad you thought of using her."

When Micki danced around, joining her, Bella was back on her journey to a perfect night with an even more perfect man.

**

Kenneth pulled up on the side of the hotel where his truck could be seen from the delivery door next to the loading dock. Any second now, Bella should be exiting from that door, escorted by the hotel manager. When he drove by the front of the hotel, he could see the large crowd gathered out front with lights flashing all over the place. It looks like they believed River was actually Bella. This would be the perfect time for Bella to run out and jump in his truck. He kept his eyes on anyone walking nearby and seeing no one, he turned when he heard the large metal door open. His heart skipped a beat when he saw Bella rushing toward him. He hopped out as fast as he could, raced around to the passenger side, opened the door to his truck and helped her get inside. Checking their surroundings again, he waved to the hotel manager, who darted back inside. Back inside of his truck, Bella was breathing as hard and fast as he was. This must be what it's like in one of her movies. He was on edge with excitement.

"We did it!" she shouted.

He laughed as she danced around in her seat, searching for the seat belt.

"We did. I need to get us away from here, but first..."

Kenneth didn't finish his sentence. He moved in her direction, reaching for and holding her face in his hands, he kissed her with all the need his body had been feigning for since their first kiss. When she sighed into the kiss, giving as good as she was getting from him, he wanted to stay like this for an eternity. There was something magical and intoxicating about kissing her. He was close to picking her up and pulling her into his lap, but he knew this wasn't the time or place to belabor the fact that they needed to get away before they were spotted.

"I hope there is more of that later," Bella pleaded, pressing her finger to where his lips had just been.

"Much more. For now, let's get moving because we have a lot to do. We're meeting Smitty's son a few miles away. Keep your hat and glasses on. I'm going to get out when we get to him, put the food in the back and hop back in. He won't see you."

"You thought of everything. I may need to pick your brain for a movie idea!" she joked.

"I have all kinds of ideas for new movies. Maybe a lot of the studios can stop with rehashing repeats and refreshing old shows and give fans new ones."

"I've been saying that also. The one thing I won't

sign on for is a rehash of an old movie, especially not one that's a pure classic."

Kenneth pulled out into traffic and dared not go anywhere near the front entrance of the hotel.

"I'm a big fan of classic movies," he said.

"Plenty at your place? I love them too."

"Then you will be in movie heaven. Classics are the best and I love that I get to introduce them to Willow. She's an old soul when it comes to music and movies," he kidded. "Ever met a nine-year-old who loves listening to Stevie Wonder, The Temptations and the Chi-lites? Those are her favorite groups. As for movies, she also loves the old black and white ones. I'm telling you, she's been here before!" he joked.

"That's hilarious. Sounds like my kind of girl. Thanks for doing this. I've been in Maryland for five months shooting this movie and for the first time, I feel like I don't have to be on point or on guard. I feel like I can literally and figuratively let my hair down. Most importantly, I'm doing it during my favorite holiday of the year, Christmas. I even dressed down like you suggested since we weren't going out."

Bella opened her long black puffy coat and when he looked inside, he saw a pink and white jogging suit and on her feet were a pair of pink and white high-top Chuck Taylor converse sneakers.

"You clearly understood the assignment," he acknowledged.

"That I did. I guess you didn't have time to

change?"

"No, I was already on the road. I will as soon as we get to my house. First up, we pick up the food and then it's on to grab the largest and most delicious milkshakes around. We'll then head for the Christmas lights until hunger overtakes us. Last, to my house where I'll park in the garage so that we still keep your presence hidden from the world because this night is all about you and disappearing for a few hours of uninterrupted peace."

"I'm all in," Bella boasted. "I love the lights I've already seen in downtown Baltimore. The city is amazingly festive."

"You haven't seen anything yet."

"The Christmas village?" she asked.

"Yeah, the one at my house!" Kenneth exclaimed and pulled off to begin their night of never-ending fun. It's been a long time for him being this excited about a date. Bella was exactly what he needed in his life this Christmas. Maybe his daughter was right after-all. He couldn't imagine anything bad about their plans.

**

Shawna Edwards paced nervously, expecting her next phone conversation to not go so well. She didn't have anything good to report. Had she been found out? How could a change be made and she not know about it? She was a member of Bella's administrative team which meant she knew everything.

She growled and stomped her feet in frustration,

pacing across the floor of her hotel room trying to calm her nerves in order to render some kind of viable excuse to a plan that has now gone awry. She nervously bit her nails knowing what his wrath would feel like. Before she could worry anymore, her phone rang.

"Well? Where are the pictures? I have hundreds of people waiting to post negative comments under those pictures on social media? What's the holdup? I expected to hear back from your guy by now?"

Shawna heaved a deep sigh.

"Brandon, I know you've been waiting but I don't have any pictures. He didn't get any."

"What do you mean he didn't get any? He did recognize her, right? Bella Hardwick is the most beautiful actress, recognizable by everyone. You said there were hundreds of people waiting and that your camera guy was able to get someone on the staff to snap a few up close and personal photos of her and this date of hers. What happened? You know I don't like being disappointed."

"I know and I'm sorry. I tried really hard. I paid him the money you sent me and he was there and ready."

"So? What happened then?" Brandon yelled.

Shawna jumped as his voice vibrated through her phone.

"She didn't show up; her movie double did. It was River Mays who got out of the car and she was alone. When she stepped out of the truck, she dramatically whipped off her sunglasses and big floppy hat, lowered the collar of her coat and then pranced around for the crowd. When people realized it wasn't Bella, they walked away and River went inside, sat down and ate dinner."

"Okay, then where is Bella and her date? I was hoping to use the photos to have people slam her and then she'll come running back to me. What makes her think she can find any guy better than me? I may not be perfect but I have to be better than this guy."

"I think you're perfect and there is no one better. I don't know where she is. The last I knew the plan was for her to meet him at the restaurant for dinner."

"Who is this guy?" Brandon asked.

Shawna was hesitant. She had already told Brandon too much, the same way she'd been doing for the past year since the night Bella sent her over to Brandon's place to deliver a gift that he'd asked her to purchase and pick up for his assistant's birthday. When she arrived, she didn't expect Brandon to open the door to his condo in the buff; he was naked and not ashamed. He was there for her to see all of him without making a move to cover himself up. She saw the sexy grin on his face he usually showed his admirers and she forgot she worked for his girlfriend. Before she knew what was happening, he had her inside of the door, up against the wall and kissing her like he'd been waiting for her all day. Her head was spinning with all kinds of visions that she'd secretly had about him since before she began working for Bella. The next thing she knew, she was ripping her own clothes off and the rest would remain a secret for the rest of her life. Brandon had been her first, something he relished knowing. Though she expected more from her first sexual encounter, the two or three minutes he did give her were more than she could have ever asked for. She found herself willing to do anything for him, including spying on Bella. What she wouldn't do was risk her job by revealing the man Bella was interested in. She wouldn't even do it for another roll in the hay with Brandon.

"I don't know that yet. She's been pretty secretive about him," she lied.

"It must be one of the actors on the set. You know, Shawna, I would do anything for you if you were able to find out who this guy is. I mean, I'll be back in Los Angeles after the New Year and I'd love to have you over. It will be our secret like the last few times. Weren't they great for you?" he asked.

"Yes," she slurred out.

"I'm thinking I could have a nice, exquisite meal cooked for us this time, like a real date. We could take a nice, hot, sexy bath together and you could be in my arms all night long. I'm talking about letting you spend the night with me. What is that worth to you? Also, I have a very special Christmas gift I bought just for you while I was in Milan. Wouldn't you like to know what it is? I will say it will look nice and shiny against your naked body. Well?"

Brandon wasn't stupid. He knew that she knew and he was buttering her up for the taking. If she didn't tell him, he may tell Bella that she's the leak on her team.

Shawna was torn. Could she betray Bella even more than she already has? Was being in Kenneth's arms worth being disloyal? If she told him and Kenneth's identity got out, she knew that could be contributed to anyone on the team or on the set of the show and not just her. It could be anybody. Everyone has seen how Bella and Kenneth look at each other like two star-crossed lovers. She wondered if they were lovers. Brandon deserved better, if Bella was cheating on him. Shawna could be what Brandon needs. All she had to do was prove herself.

"His name is Kenneth and that's all I know. He's a fireman."

"What? He's playing a fireman in the movie?" Brandon asked.

"No, he's an actual fireman. Someone local that she's fallen for."

"Wait, fallen for? I thought this was a first date or something. Is it getting serious?" he asked.

Shawna was frightened to tell him anymore. For a year, Brandon has had an upper hand on Bella and all the personal moves she tried to make and it was her fault. She liked Bella, but she was obsessed with Brandon. Every red-blooded woman in the world had the hots for Brandon, but she has actually had him. She didn't care if it was behind Bella's back or if Brandon had yet to see fit for them to make love in a bed. It was usually on the floor of his apartment, in the back of his limousine and once, recently, in the coat room at a restaurant where he was on a business meeting. He'd called her, knowing she was in Los Angeles and told her to meet him there. When she arrived, he barely said hello before slipping the maître d' a wad of money. Brandon led her to a small closet and in less than five minutes, they were done and he told her he had to get back to his dinner. Before leaving, he told her that he needed to know if Bella was planning to surprise him like she had done earlier in the year on Valentine's Day. His birthday was coming up and he had plans with another beauty and didn't want a repeat of Bella dropping in. Shawna told him that she would keep him posted and she did.

She knew she was being used, but who would enjoy being used by Brandon. He was her everything, even if he shared himself with every woman he came across.

"I think it's more serious than that."

"Shawna, what have you been hiding from me? Do I need to pay that set a visit to see what's going on?" he inquired.

She thought about how great that would be. Maybe they could spend some time together if he showed up. He can't possibly still want Bella after her eyes, and she was sure, her heart were both with another man.

"Maybe you better because I think this may really be something. I heard a rumor that someone actually saw her trailer rocking when the two of them were in it alone. You know what that means?"

Shawna knew she was wrong, but she wanted to see him. Hearing Brandon's trail of expletives on the other end, she was getting the reaction she wanted.

"Get everything you can on this guy. I need to find something to end that relationship or whatever it is. How dare she cheat on me with someone else, let alone a simple fireman. I'll teach her to try and embarrass me."

"I thought you were over her? You told me you were moving on from Bella," Shawna said. She tried to hide the sadness in her voice, but her disappointment was on the surface and her feelings were hurt to hear him pine for Bella yet again.

"I am over her, but she can be a cash cow when it comes to my career. I've used her to get where I am and staying connected to her is the key to my future endeavors in the movie world. I don't want her, but I can't have her gallivanting around with another man. That would lessen me in the eyes of the world when it came to my level of importance in her life. Find out what you can and I'll show you how I can make it worth your time when I get there. Where is this set? I need you to get access for me and a few other people. Think you can do that?"

"I can't. Bella will be mad at me."

"Just tell her that I reached out to you to surprise her and that will make up for any anger she may have.

Don't tell her up front though. It has to be a surprise. You can play innocent and I can play along to make sure you don't get in any trouble. I'll even show up with some flowers to sweeten the moment. Trust me, I don't want her. I will want you when I get there. Buy something sexy to model for me. How is that?"

Shawna smiled. All she wanted was Brandon's attention and she was about to get it. She needed to get him on the movie set and then let him take it from there. They were all using Bella in one way or another, so why should she care? She'd been jealous of Bella having Brandon's eye and now she could be where Bella was. She needed to leap at the chance.

"I'll do it. Tell me who else needs to get in. You have to make them a part of your team just in case they aren't. It should be easy to get you on with your connection to the prima-donna."

"I knew I could count on you. I'll be there as soon as I can. Could be a week or two. You're the best Shawna."

"Will I get to see you privately while you're here?" she asked, sheepishly.

"Make this happen and I got you."

Shawna hung up the phone and dialed Bella's first assistant, Micki, to see how Bella's plans for the night could change and she not be made aware.

8

Bella yawned for the tenth time as she tried with all of her might to get her lines straight for today's Christmas scene. They were coming down to the last week of shooting in Maryland before heading to Budapest in early March for the final part of the movie. The months of being in Maryland were nothing compared to the last few weeks that included the most romantic days and nights she'd ever spent. She owed it all to Kenneth and how he, with so much ease, has shown her how a woman should be treated, desired and loved. There were no dull moments in any of the time they were together whether they were playing arcade video games in his lower-level family room, relaxed watching movies with him and Willow or cooking meals together in his kitchen that most chefs would marvel at. Sneaking away with him was getting more and more trickier as people began to realize there was something going on between them.

Since their first date night two weeks ago, they were becoming inseparable. Her late-night shoots sometimes ran after midnight, to her dismay, but she could always find Kenneth on the other end of her phone checking on her day and encouraging her to get as much rest as possible. She longed to be with him, in his arms, but he kept her focused and she appreciated that. He reminded her that there was more time for them to come once shooting wrapped up. She was wondering if they could somehow make holiday plans together. She was willing to stay in Maryland a little longer if he were open to her spending Christmas and possibly New Year's with him and Willow.

Besides falling instantly in love with Kenneth, something she had yet to share with anyone, she loved her time with Willow as well. Being with them reminded her of being at home with her own family where her life in Hollywood could be left behind. She'd been thinking about that more and more since meeting Kenneth. She wanted her career, but she didn't want her career to be her life. She wanted to be in a loving relationship, to one day then have a husband and children of her own. She didn't want to start that in her forties or fifties, spending the rest of her twenties and thirties focused only on her next movie. Kenneth was showing her all kinds of ways that love is what was missing from her life. That first date gave her hope.

Trying to focus on her lines wasn't working. Bella put the script down and laid back on the chaise lounge in her trailer. The hour was extremely early and most people had yet to arrive. She had called her driver the night before and told him to pick her back up at four in the morning. She wanted to get in as much time to go over her lines as she could. Right now, all she wanted to do was reminisce on how absolutely perfect her date with Kenneth had gone that first night and every time since.

After they picked up the food he had ordered from his friend's restaurant after he carefully and strategically planned her hotel escape, they did get milkshakes, the best she'd ever had. He told her it would be. It was nice and thick, chocolatey, with the sweetest whipped cream and cherries on top. He took her on a ride through street after street in Baltimore City of rows of houses with the most dynamic light displays that she's ever seen. Those weren't million-dollar homes that paid people to put up holiday displays, but neighbors and friends who prided themselves in putting up decorations to delight children young and old. Since then, he'd taken her on more drives through more communities, some with Willow.

What she loved most about their time was how she could escape the world within the confines of his beautiful home. They were able to go there and remain unseen, even by the neighbors. She'd never felt freer.

His large single-family home was on a quiet residential street of about twenty-four homes, twelve on each side of the street. Every house had big, beautiful and quite colorful Christmas displays. Kenneth's house was no exception. There were lights everywhere, some stationary and some dazzling with all very pleasing to look at.

Once inside of is home, he took her on a tour and she loved how each room had been carefully designed in its own style and color. He said his best friend, Gabby, had helped him put it all together. His ex-wife had actually designed Willow's room. She loved that Kenneth and his ex-wife had remained good friends during and after the divorce. Together they knew the marriage wasn't working out and they didn't want to end up hating each other.

On that first date, they talked, laughed and joked while fixing their plates. They settled into the family room where he told her to act as if she were in her own home. She could put her feet up, eat on the sofa and he even allowed her to control the remote. After checking out his massive movie collection, they decided on a couple of the Star Trek motion pictures, mutual favorites of them both.

What she couldn't seem to take her eyes off of was the larger-than-life, mystical Christmas tree that almost reached the ceiling. There were Christmas balls in a variety of colors, ribbons, tinsel, lights that zoomed in a pattern around the tree. It was so gorgeous that when she found herself looking away from it, her eyes searched out for it again. The tree wasn't like any other tree that she'd ever seen. It was almost alive and speaking to her, saying the same things to her that she'd been saying to herself; she deserved more and better in life if she slowed down long enough and allowed herself to be open to it. Isn't that what she longed for? What she'd wished for? It took Kenneth coming into her life to show her that she could have it all; a career and love.

In his arms is where she found herself as they cuddled on the sofa. To her amazement, it was her who made the first move toward something more intimate between them. They were alone and unlike who she thought she was, she was indeed a woman who desired loving on a first date; a first for her. She had never desired a man as much as she desired Kenneth.

They talked about hopes and dreams, their childhoods and how they were similar and different. She told him of her life in Los Angeles and he talked about his first trip to Los Angeles when Willow was four years old. He'd taken her to Santa Monica Pier and he still remembered how her eyes lit up with excitement. When he spoke of Willow, she longed to one day be the mother of his children so that she could watch and listen to him love their children. Everything about him delighted her and the way he held her so close and tenderly, she couldn't think of a better way to spend their time together.

They kissed, caressed and loved each other for the rest of the night after he picked her up in his big, strong arms and took her to his bedroom. It was there that she experienced what real lovemaking was all about. Before Kenneth, she had been having sex. He was a man that showed her how to make love. The entire date was magical and since then, she just wanted to be with him.

Bella heard a knock on her trailer door and knew that her team had arrived for their start of the day meeting. When she opened the door, in rushed Desiree and Dana. Bella looked out of the door for the rest of the team but saw no one else; not even Micki who was usually first in the trailer each day, even before she arrived.

"The two of you beat everyone in this morning. Now that's unusual. I hope that's not a sign of snow!" Bella belted out.

"Ah ha, funny. I see you're in another good move. Does that mean that you ended up getting a late-night booty call? You did rush out of here around midnight. Was that to see Kenneth? Tell us everything!" Desiree shouted and then sat down with her head in her hands as if she were about to take in a lecture.

"No, I did not get the chance to see him last night, not that I didn't want to. I did talk to him for about an hour until I couldn't stay awake another second. I am seeing him tonight. It's Friday and I'm out of here at a decent hour for a change. I'm going through Kenneth withdrawals," she said.

"I guess that explains that hot kiss I witnessed

between the two of you the other day when you thought no one was paying attention. You're not usually the one for public displays of affection, but there you were, practically crawling up that man at his truck," Dana admitted.

"You were spying?" Bella asked.

"I wasn't spying. When you're around Kenneth, you don't even see anyone else. You are so in love with that man and it shows. I never saw you behave that way with Brandon or any other guy."

"That's because I'm an actress. I don't have to be one when I'm with Kenneth. I'm genuinely CaBella and not just Bella."

"Uh oh, she's CaBella with Kenneth! Well, damn! That's it. He's spoiled you for any other man. He must have really put something on you that first night. You said it was out of this world."

"Yes, it was. I have never experienced a sensual high like that before. It went on all-night long; I mean that literally. He's so perfect. I can talk to him about anything and she shares his thoughts and feelings with me. I feel like the CaBella you knew when we were growing up; not the Bella you see on the screen. I have to be camera ready for the world but with Kenneth, I can just be me. I didn't realize how much I needed to be that side of me until I met him. I love who I am with him. I really love me with him. I've never said that after being with anyone."

When her cell phone pinged, all three of them

looked toward her phone. Grabbing it, Bella grinned so gallantly wide that she knew Desiree and Dana had to see all of her teeth.

"Must be Kenneth. Look at that smile on her face," Desiree said.

"It's him. He's saying good morning and how much he and Willow are looking forward to having me over tonight."

"Oh, more of what happened that first night?" Dana asked.

"No way. It's the three of us tonight, not just me and him. I'm going to spend the night, but in the guest room out of respect for Willow. I'm telling you, the best thing in life is sitting with the two of them under that Christmas tree, sipping cocoa and eating popcorn. Can either of you imagine that being *me* at this point in my life? There is something about the air around this Christmas holiday that has me feeling like I'm truly living my best life. I have my family, you guys, my career and, hopefully, a kind man who lets me see who he really is; no hidden agenda. Seriously, would you ever imagine I would be excited about spending an evening with a man and his daughter?"

"No, but I like it. We're used to you jetting off to one place or another with the most high-profile people in the world. Imagining you chilling and relaxing is the furthest from where we thought you would be at this point. I speak for Dana and me when I say we're happy for you. Kenneth was exactly the man you needed to show you that men like Brandon don't warrant long-term attention."

Bella looked down at her phone at Kenneth's smiling face after receiving another text from him. She mentioned in an earlier text that today had been a rough day of filming on her body. She read through his response.

'When you get here, I'm going to prepare a hot bath, so bring your favorite girlie bath stuff. We'll then sit around the fireplace with another crab cake, which you can't seem to get enough. As you relax, I'll give your feet the perfect massage. Whatever you need, you can find it right here with me. Until I see you, close your eyes and feel my bear hug and passionate kiss and I hope that gets you through.'

She replied back that she was more than ready and then looked over at Dana and Desiree.

"I will tell you this. I'm tired of this fast life. I know I'm only twenty-eight and I should be living the high-life like other celebrities, but I don't want that. Deep down, I want a different existence, especially in my relationship. I want something that's just for me. I didn't know I needed a man like Kenneth until I did; not until he came along. I am happy."

"Well, Merry Christmas to you because we're happy for you!" Desiree shouted.

**

As the credits for the movie scrolled on the screen, Bella didn't want to give in to the sleep that was threatening to overtake her. The night had been going great and she didn't want sleep to interrupt any part of her paradise with Kenneth and Willow, though Willow was clearly out cold.

Before she arrived, Kenneth had pushed the entire sectional together, including the two large sections in the middle so that they could relax together. Willow had crawled onto the center while they watched *A Sound of Music*, one of her favorite movies. Willow had fallen asleep about half-way through when they no longer heard her singing the songs. The three of them were in their pajamas, which she had slipped on after Willow helped her get settled into the guest room. She and Kenneth wanted to be together, but they would have other times for that. Tonight, was family night.

Besides the crab cakes he'd picked up and had warming, they also cooked cheeseburgers and hotdogs on the indoor grill, with all the fixings. They baked French fries in the oven and she and Willow cut up a large bowl of fruit. After dinner, they popped popcorn and settled in around the tree.

There was that tree again, she thought. Gazing at it without looking away, she again wondered, what was it about the tree? She was more drawn to it than she should be. It made her feel good all over. It was the kind of tree that represented what it means to be family. She was experiencing perfection.

"Looks like Willow needs some help getting in bed," Kenneth said, interrupting her connection to the tree.

"Do you need some help?" she asked.

"No, you stay and find something else for us to watch. Nothing else with kids and songs, please," he joked and kissed her before getting up.

She watched him lift Willow up slowly to not wake her and head, with her in his arms, up the stairs to her room.

With him gone, she silenced the television and spoke to the tree. The tree had been calling to her since the first time she walked into the house and saw it. When she was a little girl, she and her brother would make a wish on their tree for all the toys they wanted to get. Like back then, this tree made her feel like all her dreams could come true if she wished hard enough. Could it be that easy?

"Okay, it's just you and me. What do you want from me? I hear you're magical. Is that it? Are you like, the genie in a bottle? Do you do magical things like grant wishes? There is something special about you, for sure. I noticed it the first time I saw you. You give off a vibe, almost a hum that's magnetic."

Bella looked around to see if Kenneth was returning. Not seeing him, she slid closer to the tree and whispered.

"Okay, if you're a magical tree, I have a wish. Can I have this man under my tree for the rest of my life? Is that possible? Do you have a personal connection with Santa Claus where you could plant the seed of forever for me, oh mighty tree?"

Bella laughed at herself. She was being silly, but she was also very serious about her request. She was in love with Kenneth and she didn't want a casual only relationship with him. She wanted everything with him. Miles apart didn't matter to her as long as there were airplanes to get her to him or him to her.

"Last thing – if he feels the same love for me that I feel for him, all I want for Christmas is him. All I want for Christmas now and forever is Captain Kenneth Gibson. That's it. That's the whole entire message. That's the wish. I just want him. That would make for the merriest of Christmases ever."

"Now, where were we," Kenneth said joining her.

"You're not tired?" she asked sliding back into his arms for their own personal time together.

"Not if I have to sleep alone."

Bella winked, her sign that she understood how he felt.

"I know. I've been thinking about that all day. You can't expect me to have the night with you that I had and not want that every single time I'm with you. Tonight, I'll digress and sacrifice because I don't know if I can tamper down my screams of pleasure!" she jested.

"I will settle for falling asleep right here with you in my arms, but trust, with that open invitation to have dinner in your suite, make sure you're ready for me."

Bella accepted the kiss he offered. The moment was

so sweet and sensitive and full of the two of them and what they could have.

When she turned so that she could relax again in his arms, she exhaled as he pulled her as close to him as he could, cocooned against his chest. She loved that at this moment, *Love Jones*, a movie she loved came on. She could relate because her love jones for Kenneth was strong.

Looking toward the tree again, she offered up her wish once again, this time silently. Something told her that the tree was listening. The lights seemed to twinkle a little brighter, the same way as things in her own life have brightened, all because of the man who held on to her lovingly under the Christmas tree that he called magical.

9

"Bella, you have a visitor. Shall I let him in."

Thinking it was Kenneth stopping by since she knew he was scheduled to be on-set, she excitedly raced to push past Shawna, who was blocking the doorway of her trailer, to get to him. She had a break in her day coming up and with Willow coming with him today, she was planning to enjoy her break having lunch with them.

To her dismay, on the other side of the door to her stood the last person she expected to see; Brandon. What was he doing, not just on her set, but in the country? She assumed he would go from wherever he was to then travel to Paris she thought he was still planning to spend the Christmas holiday.

"Brandon? What are you doing here?" she asked without a smile.

"Is that what I get for your man? You're not happy to see me? Baby, I'm happy to see you."

Before she could stop him, Brandon moved around

her and Shawna, bounding into her trailer. When she turned around, his cockiness was already showing as he splayed himself out across her favorite chair as if he was settling in to stay for a while. Furious, she turned to Shawna who was clearly scared near the door. She needed to be scared.

"Shawna, is there a reason I wasn't told Brandon was here? He had to get clearance through you. Is there something you failed to tell me or anyone else on the team?" she asked her.

"Don't be mad at her. I asked her to let me surprise you," Brandon offered.

"Well, I don't like surprises, do I Shawna?"

When she looked at Dana and Desiree who were still in the trailer as well, they shrugged their shoulders, letting her know that they knew nothing about his sudden appearance.

"Can you ladies give us a minute, please? I need to catch up with my baby in private, if you know what I mean," Brandon insinuated.

Bella had been caught off guard with him showing up, as well as, by him dishing out orders to her team; something she didn't like. Just like that, with him now in her space, her peace was being interrupted.

"Brandon, what are you doing here?" Bella asked again. "Stop bossing my team around," she demanded, finding and using the voice needed when dealing with him.

"Baby, I've got some good news to share with you

and it's not something I want to share with anyone else yet. I'm not bossing them around. They know how I do and so do you. I only need a few minutes. I am a little disappointed that you don't seem to be excited that I'm here to see you. You've always complained that I don't spend enough time with you and yet, I haven't even gotten as much as a hug welcoming me to this town. That's a shame considering how long it's been since I last saw you. I want to show you how much I've missed you. Listen, Shawna, can you get me a coffee, two sugars, two creams? Thanks, love."

Bella fumed, as he ignored her request. Seeing Shawna run off without question angered her even more.

"Brandon!" she shouted with annoyance.

"Now, can we talk alone?" he asked her.

Bella realized talking to him in private was a good idea. It was time she let him know that they were done for good this time. She was done with being an afterthought.

"We're leaving," Desiree said, leering at Brandon, yet smiling at her.

With them alone, Bella turned to Brandon, keeping distance between them.

"I don't appreciate you showing up like this."

"Why? You've always complained that I don't do romantic gestures. This is a big one. Surprise!" he shouted, stood and moved toward her.

"Don't touch me."

He stepped back.

"Why so cold? This isn't a happy day?"

"No, it's not."

"Don't tell me you're still made about those pictures? I can explain that."

Bella thought hard about the pictures he was making reference to. The last she remembered, they had an issue over video footage of him, not pictures.

"Pictures?" she asked.

"Yeah. I figure you must be angry about the pictures of me and that personal trainer, Allegra. That was one time and I promise you I'm done with other women."

"What are you talking about? Who is Allegra and what pictures?" she asked.

She should have known that Brandon would show up with yet another scandal following him. It was one that she had yet to hear about. She was too busy living her own happy life and not focused on his mess anymore.

"I thought that was why you were giving me the cold shoulder. Anyway, don't worry about it. Just forgive me and forget it. I'm here with you because I want you and only you. Truth be told, I think she set me up. I don't even know how someone would get a picture at that angle without it being setup that way."

"Oh, I see, another cheating scandal."

"Yeah, sort of, but you know what this life is like for us. Fans and groupies don't leave us alone."

Hearing Brandon blame others for his slipping and sliding pissed her off.

"And your lack of control or will-power has nothing to do with it. The fact that you can't seem to have happiness with one woman isn't your problem but the fault of others? Really?"

He was so cocky that she wanted to throw a chair or something at him. Dealing with his was infuriating. How could she have put herself through this for so long? How could she allow a man to not appreciate who she was or what they could be together?

"Look, you know you're going to forgive me. Let's bypass that and get to the good stuff. You know you're going to be mad for a little while and then we'll make up in our usual way. I'm saying, let's cut through that and get one in right now. I miss you and we know you miss me. Stop fighting it," he declared.

Bella could feel her skin crawling and her head about to pop with disgust.

"Are you out of your mind? You don't have any control over me! None! I am my own woman. For you to assume that I would fall back into anything is ludicrous. You are so used to missing and then dismissing me that it comes natural to you to think you have some kind of hold over me. I'm done, Brandon."

"Done? You're not done with me and you know it."

She was about to continue the fight until he jumped up, walked over to her and put his hand in front of her face to stop her in her tracks while he checked his cell phone that had just pinged. Whatever the message was, it made him smile. She started to move around him, but realized they were at the door and perhaps, she could play his game enough to get him out of her sight. He had no idea how through with him she actually was.

"Look, Bella, I know you're all emotional and everything. I'm going to be honest with you. Word reached me about this guy you've been seeing. I already know it's not serious. Did you tell him that this is what we do? When we're apart, we connect with temporary bed partners until you and I can get back together again and really knock a few out. I get it, you met this guy, he was, what cute and all? I'm fine with that, but you should really stop leading this guy on. He has no idea he's a pansy in our game of to-and-fro. I hear he's a fireman? Really? That's the best you could do. At first, I thought he was a fireman in the movie, but he's a real fireman probably barely making a decent living."

"You don't know what you're talking about," she declared defensively.

"Sugar, I know you. If you were serious about him, you would have told me about him by now. You would have called me and told me that we were through, but that's not the case. This is what we always do. You can't be happy with some fireman. You like this guy that much? Then, tell me about him. What's this guy got that makes you think you would leave me for him? What? The sex is good? What is it? He's not me, so he can't be all that."

Bella changed her mind. She wasn't going to play this game with him. For once, she wanted to keep her private life to herself. This kind of confrontation is what Brandon wants in order to make himself feel better; to feed his own personal ego. He wants to know the details so that he can scheme and come between her and Kenneth. She wasn't going to allow him to do that. For once, she was choosing to keep her growing love for Kenneth close to her heart. Brandon didn't need to be let in on that. She crossed her arms over her chest and passively responded.

"I don't know what you're talking about. I'm not seeing anyone," she stated confidently. It may be a lie, but it was one she was willing to put out in the atmosphere if it got Brandon out of her life for good. She wanted him gone and would deal with him another time. In a few short weeks, her life had changed and so had her heart. She wanted to get back to that for the time she had left in Maryland.

"No? What about this fireman? Don't try to deny it. If I'm mentioning it, I already know about him."

"Whatever you think you know isn't there. He was just someone I was passing the time with. It was nothing serious. Like you said, he's just a local fireman and he meant nothing to me at all. He was someone I connected with while I'm here, but that's over because the shoot is wrapping up in a few days. That's what we do when we're apart right? We find someone to warm our beds, but it's not real. I'm already done with him. Nothing to see or hear about here. Poof, he's gone from my life. Like I said, he never meant anything to me anyway. There you have it. Satisfied? Now, go. I have to get ready for filming today."

"See? You got your boo all worked up and I had to come visit and regulate; show my woman I love her and I'm still hers and she's still mine."

Bella pushed the air of frustration from her lungs and hoped that now that she explained what would appease him, she was ready for him to leave. She bit her tongue to keep from hitting him with the honest truth that she was in love with Kenneth who had shown her his heart and treated hers with respect. She held back her truth, hoping her lie would give Brandon the boost he needed.

"You can leave now. I have work to do and these are the last few days."

"What about this guy? Is he still hanging around? Did you let him down gently like you did other men you played this game with to make me jealous? That's why you did this, right? All this to make me pay more attention to you. Okay, I'm here. Why don't we go tell this goober together that he was wasting his time?"

"Brandon, just leave. I can do that myself. I don't need any help letting a man down. I don't know why you felt the need to come here just to beat your chest like Tarzan. Who told you anything about him and me anyway?"

He didn't know it but Brandon just provided her with proof that someone on her team was telling her personal business. This was another secret that had somehow gotten back to him. He was smug about it. She needed to find out.

"Does it matter?"

"It does to me. Someone close to me has been doing some shady stuff and I'd like to know who it is."

"Well, I'm sorry to disappoint you, but they are looking out for you and for me. This guy won't get you to the next level in your career like I can. Speaking of that, when are you joining me in Paris?"

What?" she asked. At one time that was the plan, but not anymore.

"Paris? Remember? We're spending the Christmas holiday together in Paris. I have a big surprise for you. We're going to be asked to co-host one of the biggest awards shows next year. Before you jump with joy, I have all the details and I'm only sharing them in Paris. I was asked to get you on board and trust me, if you think your career is something now, wait until all the promotion for the awards show comes out and then, at the same time, this movie you're shooting will be out and hitting the circuits. My movie will be bigger, but you know, we're a team, so it's all good. You are going to be bigger than you could ever imagine. That's if we talk about this and I get you onboard. The call is yours if your career is worth you being on stage with me. I'm doing it no matter what. I tossed out the idea of us doing it together and the power behind this loves it."

"Why haven't my people been told? I haven't seen anything from my agent about this," Bella declared.

"That's because this is all still contingent on you and I coming to an understanding. I want to be sure you've ended this foolishness with the fireman. We have an image as a couple to keep up. Your days of him being your plaything while in this cold ass town is over and done. That is, if you want to hear more about this opportunity. You are first on my list, but you're not the only woman superstar on my list."

Bella hated being in Brandon's clutches and little does he know that she doesn't care about any opportunity. She cares about how she's been feeling since meeting Kenneth. Brandon was fishing and she wasn't about to bite the hook.

"I'll think about it. Right now, I have to get back on set."

"Not to see lover boy, though, right? You're done with him for sure?" he asked.

"I told you he never meant anything to me. It was fun and now it's over. I'm leaving in a few days and I'll never see him again."

"Oh, he was nothing to you? That's good to hear! His name is Kenneth, right? He was just someone you wet your whistle with. I knew it. He could never be more than that. Hell, he's just a little ol' fireman," Brandon shouted.

Bella looked at him sideways. He was talking

louder than he needed to considering it was only the two of them in her trailer. It was also strange that he was talking more at the door than to her. She brushed it off because she no longer cared. If her agreeing with everything he says would get him out of the door faster, she would agree to anything.

"Okay, yes whatever."

"Then, I can leave and make my way to Paris to set everything up for a romantic holiday together. Wait until you see the chalet I have for us. It's got a huge king-size bed and a tub made for two. We have a lot of making up to do. I assume I should expect you in three days, then?" he asked.

Why was he still talking so loud and not even looking at her? He was so loud and focused on what he was saying that she was sure he didn't hear the tone of her voice; the one that was actually saying she wasn't meeting him anyplace in three days. She didn't know what he was up to practically yelling, but she was ready for it. What she needed most was distance.

Seeing Brandon reminded her of what she had with Kenneth. There was a time when she thought she was in love with Brandon, but that's not what it was. Everything that is Kenneth is real, true love. What she felt for him encompassed her very being. Just thinking about him made her smile. To be in love during the Christmas season was magical in itself. She was in love and she couldn't wait to tell Kenneth how she felt. She didn't want to scare him off with confessions of love after three weeks, but she'd never felt this way before and she never wanted to let go of it.

"Okay, three days, Brandon. Now, leave so that I can get back to work."

Bella tried to push him through the door to get him out of her trailer faster, but he planted his feet and wouldn't move.

"Sure, let me escort you out," he finally said. "Three days and we'll be making love all over Paris and you can forget about this guy you used to get to me right?" he said.

Bella wasn't paying attention to her surroundings. She looked behind her to make sure she wasn't leaving anything.

"Yeah, sure. Now, go!" she demanded.

When she finally stepped out on the top step of her trailer, Bella looked around and saw a crowd of people and quickly wondered why they were standing around staring. She looked for her security and then remembered they weren't needed with her today. Even if they were, they wouldn't have put up much of a fuss over Brandon's sudden arrival. They knew who he was. He traveled with an entourage who would have been cleared by her own team, so her guys wouldn't have squawked at that either. They were familiar with seeing everyone in attendance from her production team, to her administrative team to Kenneth and Willow. The look on Kenneth's face told a myriad of stories. She locked eyes with him and knew what had just happened. She was horrified.

"You were saying?" Brandon asked. She watched him moved down the steps to the ground. She did not miss the humor in his voice. She'd been set up. The same way he tried to say groupies were always setting him up, he'd managed to do the same to her and she missed it.

Where had all these people come from and why were they standing outside of her trailer as if they were watching a movie?

"What's going on?" she asked with a shaky voice.

"What's going on is our audience, sweetheart. You know what that is, right? Isn't that why your antics drew me here? You like the attention as much as I do."

Bella wanted attention from one person and it just so happens that the one person she wanted was glaring at her as if she were someone he didn't know. Then it clicked for her. In a matter of seconds, her mind went back over her conversation with Brandon when they were inside of the trailer. She understood his desire to talk louder than usual. He wanted everyone standing around to hear what they were saying, especially Kenneth.

His eyes told her everything she needed to know. Kenneth had not been privy to her need to get rid of Brandon by any means necessary. There was no way he would understand what she said and why she said it. His face told her everything that was said had landed on him like a ton of bricks. Not only was he standing there, but so was Willow and the look on her face was one that Bella never, ever wanted to see. The little girl was hurt. Willow looked like she was about to cry and Bella's heart sank. She may not have understood all that was said, but she knew that the words she heard had hurt her father.

Her heart hurt for what they must be going through, hearing her speak dismissive of Kenneth. She wanted to go to them, but then cameras started flashing. Brandon had brought an audience with him. She didn't recognize any of those people. Looking around wishing and praying that the ground would open up and swallow her whole, she saw Shawna who stood looking as if she had a secret, gazing around aimlessly, but wouldn't look her way.

"Brandon? What have you done? What did you do and why?" she pleaded, finally coming down the few steps.

She was speaking to Brandon but her eyes stayed on Kenneth as she moved in his direction.

"I thought it was time that your fella here understood that what the two of you had was only temporary."

When Kenneth took a few steps back and away from her, she stopped moving. Now was not the time; at least not with an audience and his daughter now in the midst of the *Brandon Show*. This was classic him. He had to go all out to make a point and this time, there were casualties; they were Kenneth and Willow.

"Are you completely crazy? This is going too far, even for you."

"Is it? Did you not just say that you would see me in three days in Paris? I even mentioned some activities and you didn't disagree. Deal with it, sugar! This is what we always do. I allow you your playthings but then you always come back to me."

"Brandon! Shut up! There is a child present. Are you really this insane? Are you this much of a control freak? Get out of here, now, and take your circus with you!" Bella screamed. "Kenneth, I can explain," she added.

She tried moving in his direction again and this time, he put his hand up to stop her. Before she could say another word, he picked up Willow and walked away as swiftly as he could. As much as she wanted to go to him, Willow was the most important. He was right to whisk his daughter away from Brandon's madness. Until he left, things would only get worse. She turned her fury to him.

"How dare you?" she yelled, louder this time.

"How dare I what? This is us. We do this for the cameras. Think of what the blogs will talk about tomorrow," he professed loudly.

"You are a vile human being. There is no us. This isn't what we do. There was a child present for all of this. You are out of your damn mind!"

"But your man was present too. He had the perfect view and was in perfect ear range to hear that you weren't serious about him. It's a shame I had to do all of this to remind you of who I am and the image we need to keep up."

"Oh, like the image you continually keep up with all the women you bed?"

"What was this with that guy? Was it a tit-for-tat? You bed a guy because I love women? Women can't play the same games we men play. You should know that by now."

"Go away Brandon. I never want to see you again. You've gone too far. You just hurt someone I really care about."

"I didn't hurt him, you did. Did you already forget what you said in response to my questions? Were you lying to me or to him? Do you even know? We'll bounce back just as we always do. When you get to Paris, I promise I'll turn over a new leaf. No more bed buddies for you, though. I don't like it. It bothers Brandon's ego; just a little though."

He's speaking in third person now? Everything she ever thought about Brandon that she tried to push away was true. She was no longer going to torture herself with him. She wants better. She's known better.

"You know what, you're a sad person, Brandon. You have to go through this whole orchestrated performance to what, embarrass me? To prove some point? His daughter. She's nine years old and think of what she heard."

"Well, that wasn't my plan and I'm sorry for that.

I'm not completely heartless. When I asked Shawna to make sure he was here, I didn't realize he'd have a kid with him."

Bella's head snapped around so hard in Shawna's direction, that she knew she'd feel that pain in her neck later. The look in Kenneth's eyes told her that his usual massages would not be coming her way anymore.

"Shawna? What did you do?" she lamented.

Bella watched Brandon raise his hand as if he were a student in school needing to ask a question of the teacher.

"I can answer that. Poor Shawna here is stupid enough to have been an inside person for me when it comes to your happenings for a long time; over a year. I've proved my point, so I don't need her anymore. It's been fun, though, right Shawna?"

Brandon licked his lips and winked at Shawna. Bella cringed. She knew that look and that movement of his tongue. He was letting her know that Shawna had been drawn into his world and she knew how he'd done it.

"Shawna. What did you do?" she asked her again.

Bella exhaled and looked her way and saw tears in Shawna's eyes. She'd been lured into Brandon's web, something Bella knew all too well.

"Bella, I'm sorry," Shawna cried.

Brandon's sinister laughter behind them drew her attention.

"You're apologizing now? What about that night

when you came to my home bearing more than the gift Bella asked you to deliver? Why don't you tell her what else you delivered to me?" Brandon said snidely.

"Stop it, Brandon," Bella said. Shawna may have betrayed her but she wouldn't allow him to belittle her this way. Shawna was definitely fired, but allowing him to treat her the way he does all women who fall under his devious spell, she would not allow.

"Stop what? I'm just saying that you should watch the company you keep. She was willing to do anything for me, including betray you. Oh, sorry Shawna. Your plans for visiting me in my hotel room tonight are off. I need to keep my energy for when Bella joins me in Paris. Isn't that right, honey?"

Bella started to respond until she saw Brandon pose in various ways for the cameras that continued to flick away. When he reached for her, she slapped his hand away.

"Don't touch me! Don't you ever touch me again."

Out of nowhere, like ninja's, her security team leaped into action and lifted Brandon high with the intent to drop him cold to the ground if she wanted them too.

Just then Desiree walked up.

"What's going on here?" she asked.

Bella watched Kenneth struggle against being held and when his own two security guys thought to intervene, they backed off knowing they were no match for the men she had in place.

"Brandon here put on a show in front of Kenneth and I fell for it. I said some things I didn't mean to say all to get rid of Brandon and Kenneth heard me; so did Willow."

Saying his name, Bella looked for where Kenneth had gone off too. She needed to talk to him before he left or he would never forgive her.

She turned back to see Desiree addressing the security team.

"Guys, get this trash off of the lot and I don't care who he is, if he shows up again, have him arrested for trespassing. I would say take his picture to remember his face, but it's not hard to remember what a snake looks like," Desiree warned.

Bella watched Brandon raise his hands in surrender as her guys escorted him and his followers away. That was the first time her security team had been caught off-guard, all because of her relationship with Brandon. He'd always been able to come and go. She would make sure that from this point forward, he would never get within any range that she wouldn't allow a perfect stranger to do. She was done with him. From the look on Kenneth's face, she had a feeling he was done with her.

"Merry Christmas, my Bella!" Brandon shouted as he was being dragged off. She would love to see a picture of that online.

Unlike her character, she gave him the finger and it felt good. She would say the words that went with the finger, but she was a lady first.

She turned to see her other two assistants running up, followed by extra security and her agent, Alicia. Pulling up the rear was Dana who rushed over to her.

"Are you alright? Desiree texted that I needed to get here immediately. I was close by. What's going on?" Dana asked.

"Brandon happened."

Bella knew she didn't need to say much more. His name was enough.

"What can I do?" Desiree asked.

Bella turned to Denim who walked over to Shawna who was crying profusely. As much as she wanted to have compassion for a woman who fell for the games Brandon likes to play, she had to think of her own safety and what Shawna had done. She couldn't keep anyone around she couldn't trust.

"Denim? Take all of Shawna's credentials and see that she's on her way to the airport and home immediately. She's fired."

"Bella, what gives?" her agent asked.

"Too much to get into right now."

"Bella, I don't know what's happening here, but you're due on set. You have a schedule to keep," Felix, her assistant on-set said.

"I'm on my way."

"You're good?" Desiree asked.

"I have to be. I have to get through this and then I need to speak to Kenneth. These last three days are hectic with wrapping up my scenes before the holiday."

"Was it bad?" Desiree whispered.

"Tragic and it's all my fault. When I think of what I said and what Kenneth may have heard, I don't think he's going to want to talk to me anymore."

"Ugh, I cannot stand Brandon. When I saw all these people following him around, I thought you knew he was coming or I would have been here. Shawna said you had arranged for him to have access to the set."

"I now know why he was able to have so many insights into my life when he wasn't around. I'm thinking of all the times he questioned me about stuff that he should not have known about."

"You said you thought you had a spy in your camp. Do you think she's the only one?"

"I don't but at this moment, I don't care. I care about finishing up this movie and figuring out if I have any kind of a future with Kenneth."

"Bella?" Felix called out to her.

Bella left without saying another word. The woes of being an actress had just hit her in the face. Despite the drama around her, she had to first take it to the set while her personal life had to wait; which meant, Kenneth had to wait. She only hoped that he would wait and hopefully forgive what he heard. Despite what had just happened, she was still believing in the magic of his tree. She was still wishing on it and hoping for her on happily ever after.

As she walked, she contemplated what her life

would be like without Kenneth and Willow in it and she didn't like what she saw.

"I wished on a tree," she mumbled. "I wished on a tree."

This was not the Merry Christmas she'd hoped and wished on. Was what she shared with Kenneth salvageable? If that Christmas tree was truly magic, she would find away. She only needed a sign.

10
Christmas Eve

"Get off the phone and go to him. You are still in Maryland for a reason. I was expecting to call you and hear that you were already back home."

Bella sat in the arm chair after pulling it close to the window overlooking the Baltimore Inner Harbor from her vantage point at the Harbor East Four Seasons Hotel. This was her third night here and she was still as lonely as she had been the first night she had moved here from the hotel where she'd been staying since she arrived. Fans and paparazzi were overwhelming her and the staff at the other hotel and she needed some peace. Thanks to some maneuvering, she was able to anonymously get another suite after deciding that she wasn't quite ready to head home yet. The rest of those working on the movie had already gone home, including Desiree who was now on the phone.

"I couldn't leave. I tried and I couldn't. Can you believe I only met him three weeks ago and I feel a sense of anxiety at the thought of leaving without seeing him? I was so mean and so Hollywood-*ish*, all to put on a show for Brandon, who couldn't give two shakes about me; not really. I mean, I know he cares, but not enough; not like Kenneth."

"Girl! You are whipped like I've never seen you before. I know you said the few times the two of you were intimate was mind-blowing, but you're acting like you can't live without him. What's going on?" Desiree asked.

"Don't laugh at me or think I'm crazy, okay?"

"I would never do that unless we were joking about something. Your voice sounds serious. Do we need to facetime?"

"No, no, I'm good. I just need to get this out and then decide what to do."

"Hit me with it."

"I love him. I'm in love with Kenneth."

"You're what?" Desiree yelled.

"You heard me. I've been sitting here since you and Dana left and what's keeping me here is I'm in love with him. I don't want to walk away from what I feel when I'm with him. He made me feel so good and I'm not just talking about intimacy. That was as mind-blowing as I said it was, but it's more than that. My heart aches thinking about not being with him. When I think about getting on that plane, I get nervous."

"I was the first to tell you that there was something about him that you would like. I'm going to say this to you now, not as your employee, but as your best friend – don't you dare let that man get away. Are you trying to weigh being with him against being with Brandon? Because if so, there is no comparison. I've always been honest with you. That's why we have been best friends for so long. I'm never going to sugarcoat anything. I have never liked how Brandon treats you like you're arm candy to help boost his career. He cheats on you, disrespects you and leaks your private moments to the media to get him more likes, sympathy and hits on his social media. You are in Hollywood, but you are not made of Hollywood. Brandon could never give you want you really desire."

Bella nodded her head though Desiree couldn't see it. She was glad her friend couldn't see the tears that flowed down her cheeks. She spent so much time doing things to please and make everyone else around her happy that she didn't take the time to seek out and have what made her happy.

"I want what you have and what Dana has and what so many other women have. I want a man who loves, adores and cherishes me without caring how much money I have or how many movies I've made. Brandon just wants to have fun and not once have we ever talked about anything other than how to make our careers bigger and better. I was in Kenneth's arms and it felt like home; it felt like forever. It felt like what I've always wanted in a man. I mistreated him by the words I spoke that day and I've been regretting them since they came out of my mouth. When I opened that door and saw him and Willow standing there, I've never felt lower and more disgusted at myself. I let Brandon make a show, a play for the media. I fell for it. I was so used to playing these games with him that, for a second, I didn't think of Kenneth and then, there he was, hearing it all. I can't let it end like that. What we shared was special; it was sweet; it was endearing and it was the best three weeks of my entire life. I want Kenneth. I need him, Desi."

"You're serious. You called me Desi. Only you call me that and it's when you're speaking from a place deep within where a friend like me would understand. You think you're broken, but you're not. You're in love and you think you've hurt him like Brandon has done to you so many, many times. It's not the same. You didn't mean it. You're not that kind of person. It's okay to feel this way. It's okay to feel bad when you've hurt someone you love."

And then it happened. Bella tried to hold in her cry and she couldn't. She could have been with Kenneth right now, but instead, she was, again, in a hotel alone, watching her social media and blog shows and hearing her own words thrown back at her again and again from the video that Brandon leaked of their encounter on her set. She was thankful that there was no recording of the look on Kenneth's face or Willow's.

She would have never forgiven herself if so.

Her cries became so loud that she could hear Desiree on the other end saying she was flying back to Maryland immediately and she didn't care that it was Christmas Eve.

"Bella, listen to me. It's going to be okay. Everything will be okay. I'm going to see how fast I can get a flight out and I'll be there before you know it. If you want to come here, you know you're more than welcome. I can't leave you like this by yourself on Christmas Eve in tears. Don't do this to yourself. What Brandon did isn't worth shedding one tear over. Yes, losing Kenneth is worth every tear you have. You can remedy that. You're still in Maryland. Go see him. Have you tried calling him?"

She tried to answer, but the tears wouldn't stop flowing. When she finally let out a piercing wail, letting go of the pain she'd been feeling for days, she sat up and worked on pulling herself together.

"I'm okay," she said, not just to Desiree but to herself. She needed to let that cry that she'd been holding in out. She needed to release that so that she could think clearer about what to do next.

"I'm coming. Just hold tight. Baby, I need you to get me a flight out right now."

Bella heard Desiree talking to her wife in the background.

"No, no, don't you dare. It's Christmas Eve and you should be with your family. I'm going to be alright. I needed to get that out and I needed to talk to you. No, I haven't called him and he hasn't called or texted me. I've been checking my phone for three days."

"Okay, he hasn't reached out. He probably thinks you're done with him. There is nothing preventing you from calling him. You stayed there for a reason. You switched hotels to stay there in peace when you could have easily flown home, you know like E.T. did in that movie you love."

Bella laughed so hard, she forgot she was just crying.

"Uh, I needed your humor. What if he doesn't want to talk to me or see me? You heard what I said and you saw his reaction."

"We all saw his reaction and then he took his daughter and left. I wish that wasn't the last day on set or he would have had to return and you could have explained yourself to him. You can either leave and go home and not have Kenneth or you can stay there and try to work it out. You always run. Don't do that this time."

"What do you mean I always run?"

"Every time Brandon did his dirt, you ran and secluded yourself away from the public eye until things blew over. Then, you would go back to your life like nothing happened. You weren't happy with Brandon. He was comfortable for the life you were in. I told you one day, you would come across the perfect man and he would not be in the industry. You didn't think you could see yourself with someone not in the same line of work as you. You didn't think you would be happy, but look at you. I watched you with Kenneth since day one and you were practically walking on air. Your scenes were perfect, with hardly any second takes. You were on it."

"That's because I wanted to hurry up and spend time with Kenneth."

"See? You've never, ever done that before. You never focused on life after each day of filming. Don't you dare give up on having something with him if you think it could lead to something really special. So, what he's a fireman."

"You know that has nothing to do with anything. That man is perfect in every way. He could be the man bringing us lunch every day as long as the heart he has comes with him. I felt an instant vibe with him and he felt it too. We connected and it was damn near perfect. Then I had to go and mess it up. I swear, I am my own enemy, messing up my own life. I can't blame this on Brandon. He is who he has always been."

"I bet he's in Paris right now wondering when your plane is going to land. I bet he thinks with a few days, you would run back into his arms again. I'm happy that he will be disappointed. It's time you stopped trying to make an impossible relationship with him possible on his terms. You deserve so much more. You deserve a good man like Kenneth. Everyone on the movie set loved him and his daughter."

"I love them too."

"Then fight for them. Are you sure you don't need me? You know I would swim an ocean to get to you, my friend. That's the kind of friend you have in me. Just say the word and I'll have my ticket in hand and on my way to the airport."

"No, I'm good. I just needed to talk to you, my voice of reason. I know what I'm going to do."

"I hope it's something good, delicious and fun with that hunky man. That brother is some kind of fine."

"Yes, he is and you know what, he's all mine."

"Yeah! Get your man and call me with your plans. I need to know if you're going home or staying in Maryland even longer. I'm voting and praying for Maryland. I'm going to send you positive vibes that this will work out in your favor. You with me?" Desiree asked.

"I'm with you. I'll call you later."

"Don't forget. I'll be waiting."

"I won't forget. Thank you for being my friend; for being my best friend. Merry Christmas, Desiree. I love you, sis."

"I love you, too. Now, go on and love all on that sexiness. I have no doubt he'll understand when you explain."

"Keep those good vibes coming!"

Bella hung up and rushed around her room, gathering her things and called for her driver, David, to pick her up. He had already been waiting on her call to take her to the airport for her private flight to Los Angeles. She needed to get up the nerve to have him make a detour that could make or break her life. She had to try. She had to see if what she and Kenneth had was real to them both or just her. She'd never visited him uninvited, but tonight, she was hoping and praying and still wishing on a tree that he would give her a chance to explain and hopefully forgive her.

"Alright tree – I'm still counting on you to work your magic.

11

Bella twitched nervously in the back of the Navigator truck she'd been using since she arrived in Maryland. David would look at her through the rearview mirror every couple of minutes, expecting her to change her mind on her destination as she had done four times already. She loved how he didn't question her as she changed her mind again and again. He simply made turn after turn based on her request.

When they first left her hotel, her instruction was to take her to Kenneth's house and within a block, she lost her courage and asked him to take her to the airport. In a few short minutes, she had talked herself out of, what could be, an embarrassing moment if Kenneth slammed his front door in her face. Exhaling and realizing she didn't want to be that person, she resigned herself to trying to be happy about going home and putting the entire stay in Maryland behind her.

Smiling, she found herself looking forward to her private jet to Los Angeles where she could wallow in self-pity for once again, making the wrong choice which ended what could have been the perfect relationship. She let an ex get in her head and now the man that snowy nights like this were meant to be spent with was the furthest from wanting to be in her presence as she could get.

"How could I have been so stupid!" she yelled at herself, yet again.

When David attempted to inquire, she put her hand up to stop him. She wasn't losing her mind by talking to herself. She was merely kicking herself for always ending up in this position.

As soon as David made his way through evening traffic to get onto the beltway, she experienced a panic attack which stole her breath away. The more she thought of not fighting for love, she knew running, as Desiree said she often did, was not the answer. Door slammed in her face or not, she needed Kenneth to hear her out. She also needed to apologize for Willow.

As they rounded the bend to turn onto Kenneth's street, she held onto her nerve knowing she had to do this whether it turned out good or bad for her. What she was about to do, she never thought she'd come down off of her high-horse long enough to do.

As the truck pulled onto the familiar street, she saw the house lit up in the dark night sky with lights twinkling from around the outside of the house, to the windows and also around the yard where she saw a Santa and his reindeer as well as the large tree in the front yard lit up from the very top to the very bottom. This was Kenneth's house. The few times she'd been here, she admired everything about his decorating technique, all to make sure his daughter had the perfect Christmas experience. She remembered how her own father did the same when she was a little girl.

Growing up, she had a perfect life and that was before money and fame entered the picture. Life was good and simple with no stresses. That's what Kenneth offered her; a safe place to just be herself without cameras and fanfare. For the first time in her life, she went to bed at night and woke up in the morning in the arms of a man who wanted her for her and nothing else. He thought himself unworthy of her while the entire time, she hadn't treated him like she was worthy of him. She'd fallen in love with a hero in three weeks and before she got on any plane going anywhere, she needed to see him one last time, if that was all he would give her. He needed to know how she really felt about him.

When the truck stopped in front of his house, she prayed softly to herself.

"God and Santa, please soften Kenneth's heart and let him see my true feelings and not those of a woman trying to put on a façade. Let him see me and not a character acting out a role. Let him believe me when I say that I love him. Let this be my best Christmas ever with the best possible man ever. Amen."

"Amen," her driver said.

"Thank you, David. I'll be back. Can you check to be sure my flight is leaving though I'm running late? Kenneth may toss me out on my head and if that's the case, I need to get out of here as soon as possible."

"I don't think you'll need that flight, but just in case, as you say, I sure will. Make sure you let me know if things turn out well and you want me to leave you here."

"I'm sorry I'm keeping you this late on Christmas Eve. I know you have a family you want to get home to."

"Don't you worry about me. I've got the love of my life waiting for me at home no matter what time I get there. After thirty years of marriage, we don't sweat the small stull like me working late. It's the time we spend together that counts. Besides, I love happy endings and something tells me, that's exactly what's about to happen for you. You do what you need to do. Feel free to grovel. I know that's a lot for you Hollywood types, but it works on us average people," he said, smiling and giving her a thumbs up.

When David winked at her, she felt empowered that she could do this.

Getting out, she felt the cold chilly night and was happy she chose to put on her white furry boots to match her long white coat and fur hat. She shivered against the blistering cold and raced to the front door. Inhaling, she gathered her nerve and rang the bell.

After a few seconds went by, she rang it again and this time the front door opened. On the other side wasn't Kenneth but a very beautiful woman with Willow at her side. Had he already moved on from her? She held her composure and self-confidence.

"Hello, is Kenneth here?" she asked the woman. She then looked down into the face of the little girl who usually had a smile when she saw her. That's not what Bella encountered.

"Hi, Willow."

"Hi, Ms. Hardwick."

"Miss Bella. You used to call me Miss Bella," she said.

"That was before you hurt my daddy. You treated him bad and that wasn't nice," Willow bemoaned.

"Willow Gibson!" Gabby exclaimed. "That wasn't a nice thing to say at all. Apologize right this instant. You have been taught better."

Bella watched the exchanged and hated that she'd caused it by her presence.

"But she did hurt him. Didn't daddy tell you the mean thing she said? Daddy told me to never talk about people like that. Daddy was upset."

"I said apologize and stay out of grown people stuff," Gabby said.

"It's okay. She doesn't have to because she's right. I said some terrible things and I shouldn't have, considering I didn't mean them. I was lashing out at my ex-boyfriend who was trying to embarrass me and what

I had going on with Kenneth was caught in the crossfire. I was hoping to talk to him before I left tonight."

"I understand, but still, Willow needs to apologize and then go sit down. Now!" Gabby said sternly, looking down at Willow, giving her a look that meant business.

"I'm sorry Miss Bella. That wasn't nice. I apologize for what I said."

"Now, go sit down and check that mouth," Gabby demanded."

As Willow walked away with her head down, Bella felt even worse. She had been mean to Kenneth and now, she was responsible for Willow getting in trouble.

"I'm sorry, she can be brutally honest. She gets that from a little bit of me and her father."

"Oh, are you his ex-wife, Carrie?" Bella asked.

"No," was all Gabby said. She didn't want to get into a long discussion about who she was unless asked.

"Oh, okay. I take it you may be someone Kenneth is seeing? I don't mean to intrude. Don't even tell him I was here. I'm sorry that I came here."

Bella turned to head back to the car.

"Wait! Come back," the woman called to her.

She turned and headed back to the front door.

"Yes?" she asked.

"Come inside the house for a minute."

She stepped inside and shook off the cold. From where she stood, she could see Willow standing in the middle of the family room with her arms folded across her chest with a frown on her face. Bella didn't think about the impact of what she said and how it would affect Willow who had been front and center for the Brandon debacle. Since then, her only thought had been on how Kenneth was thinking. She hated herself that Willow was a casualty of her selfishness.

"I'm sorry Willow is upset," she admitted. "I never meant for any of this."

"That little girl loves her daddy with everything in her. To correct you, I'm not someone that Kenneth is seeing. I'm Gabby or Gabriella, Willow's godmother and Kenneth's best friend."

"Oh, yes, he's spoken of you a lot of times. I'm sorry for assuming."

"It's okay. It's not the first time nor will it be the last. Happens all the time. Kenneth isn't here. He got a call from the station house a few hours ago and he's been there ever since. I do expect him back soon if you want to wait around. He would never miss Christmas morning with Willow. There was a big giveaway at the firehouse tonight and they needed extra hands to put together bikes and other toys for single mothers with children who don't have anyone to help assemble stuff."

Bella nodded.

"Right, because that's the kind of good, no, great, man Kenneth is. I've been so stupid. I'm supposed to be on a plane back home but I couldn't go until I talked to him. I'm so sorry for how things turned out. I was hoping he would consider forgiving me. I can't leave like this, with him angry at me for my foolishness. That's not me at all. He's an honorable man and every woman would be lucky to have caught his eye. I took it for granted."

She was rambling. There was a chance that Gabby didn't even know what she was talking about. Had Kenneth told her?

"If you're wondering if I know, yes, I do. Under any other circumstance, I would be cursing you out right now for what he told me you said. As a woman, I think I understand."

Bella exhaled, happy that she wasn't on the end of a tongue lashing. She was still reeling from the one Willow gave her.

"I didn't mean a word of it; not one single word. I as trying to get myself out of a jam and away from Brandon."

"Ah, Brandon. He's cute, but not worthy of a good woman. Bella, we've all been there. I do know that Kenneth was extremely upset but he truly cares about you. He wouldn't want you to leave without the two of you having a chance to talk. He doesn't give his heart away easily, but I get the feeling that's exactly what he did with you. We talked and I don't usually share about our talks, but for this one time, I will. After we talked earlier today and he had a chance to calm down, he said he got it. He is also the typical man and is saving face.

My other half, Ray, is just like that. Kenneth doesn't know whether to reach out to you or not. He wants to but he's not sure what he'll get. He's not sure who he'll get; the Bella he's fallen for or the one who plays games of the heart with her rich boyfriend."

"Ex-boyfriend. He was that when I started seeing Kenneth and he still is."

"You and Kenneth need to talk."

Bella smiled.

"I hope you're right because I sat in my hotel room for the past few days after taping wrapped up and all I thought about was him. I should have left here days ago, but I couldn't. I realized that in the short time that I've known him, I've fallen in love with everything about him; and I do mean everything. That's never happened to me before."

"In your line of work and with your unmistakable beauty, men fall at your feet all the time. They find you desirable and I'm sure Kenneth did as well, but I know him and that wasn't the only thing that drew him to you. His heart is on his sleeve."

"Would I be overstepping if I asked you for the address to the firehouse? I really need to see him. I don't want to go home with hurt between us; not when all I want to do is love him and have him love me."

"You can have any man you want – are you sure it's Kenneth?"

"There is no doubt in any part of me. I swear on that big beautiful Christmas tree that I am in love with him. He's all I want. I knew it that day and I know it now. My problem is, I've never felt this kind of love for anyone before. He is something special and I can't lose that. I just want to love him and Willow."

"Listen, I don't want to doubt what you're feeling, but Kenneth is the closest to a brother that I've ever had. I've always been overprotective of him which is where Willow gets it from. The woman who gets his heart should appreciate him. He's not flashy or chasing fame and fortune. He's a man who loves his family, loves his daughter and if I'm correct, he loves you too. If I'm right, don't take that for granted. I've seen these Hollywood relationships and how flighty they can be, no disrespect, but that's not him at all."

"I understand. My life has been an open book and most of it, as far as relationships, has been a trainwreck. When I met Kenneth and spent time with him, my eyes were open to the kind of good man I've always wanted. In a matter of weeks, he became that and more. I love him and I never want to hurt him. I want to talk to him and explain. I need to apologize for my behavior and hope and pray that he'll be able to see my true heart."

Bella waited as Gabby eyed her from head to toe, no doubt, looking for something that countered the words that she spoke. Bella knew she wasn't going to find anything. She wanted Kenneth and if he still wanted her, she would have the greatest Christmas gift of all; the right man.

"Your phone?" Gabby asked, holding out her hand.

Bella unlocked her cell phone with her password and freely handed it over to her. She watched as Gabby pecked away on the keys before handing the phone back.

"That's the address to the firehouse. I suspect he'll be there for at least another hour. He still has a lot to do around here tonight, if you know what I mean."

Bella nodded her head knowing that she meant he needed to get home and eventually get Christmas ready for Willow in the morning.

"I really appreciate this. I'm happy I got the chance to meet you. Kenneth spoke highly of you and the bond you share. I hope we will get to see each other again. I will owe you something for helping me out this way."

Gabby leaned close to her.

"Think you can get me tickets to the next Coachella event? Those tickets are hard to get."

Bella laughed out loud and winked at Willow who was still watching them.

When Willow smiled and winked back, that gesture made her heart melt. She loved that little girl as much as if she were her own. If she played her cards right, perhaps one day she and Kenneth would have more children. She then turned her attention back to Gabby.

"I'll do you one even better. I'll not only get you tickets to Coachella, which is an easy request, but when you go, you can stay at my house and my driver will get you back and forth. You won't have to worry about drinking and driving."

"Oh, you know me so well."

"I'm hoping I can say that Kenneth and I would love to go also."

"I know the man I call my brother from another mother and if you're open and honest with him, that forgiving heart of his will embrace you and forgive anything that happened between you that may have caused division."

Bella placed her phone back in her bag and turned toward the door.

"From your lips to Santa's ears," she said before Gabby opened the door for her.

"The tree, right?" Gabby asked.

"I made a wish," she admitted.

"So did Willow."

"The tree knows," Bella said turning toward the road where David sat idling in the car.

Trudging back out into the cold, Bella raced to the car as David came around and opened the door for her. Once inside and after he was back behind the driver's seat, she gave him the address of where she needed to be. Her destiny awaits. Thanks to Gabby, she was feeling good about her decision to stay.

12

“Hey, Captain, there’s a woman here to see you.”

Kenneth looked up from where he sat behind his desk to find Tyler, one of the house trainees, standing in the doorway. Coming to the firehouse on Christmas Eve was not his original plan for being off for the holiday, but sitting at home wallowing over his short, brief, but magical time with Bella wasn’t his idea of how he wanted to spend Christmas Eve either. When he heard that more help was needed and Gabby was already at his house wrapping her own gifts for her boyfriend, Ray, he decided to go help out here. That also gave Willow time to wrap the extra gifts she bought for him when Gabby took her out shopping the day before.

When the firehouse put out the call for more volunteers, he didn’t expect to arrive to find an additional forty or so men helping with putting toys together and stuffing the many large gift bags they had to give out. With that much help, he separated himself from the group and found a few things in his office he wanted to look over. Just when he was enjoying the solitude, Tyler appeared in his doorway talking about a woman.

"There are a lot of women here. We're wrapping up a toy drive and a plethora of other women, including female firefighters who came out to help are here. Besides, other women have been coming by all day, from what I'm told, asking for more help with gifts for kids this year."

"I know, but this is a special woman. *Really* special," he stressed.

Watching Tyler sway from side to side was getting annoying. At twenty, he was the youngest at the station and the most eager. He was also the runner for the firefighters.

"Why are you acting so strange? This can't be the first time you've seen a woman."

Kenneth laughed at his own joke as he went back to looking over the papers on his desk.

"You will want to talk to this woman yourself. Trust me, Cap," Tyler beamed.

"Have Norm find out what she wants," he added. When Tyler didn't move, he looked his way again.

"No can do. I was told to get you. Norm told me to not come back unless I had you with me."

He looked up and Tyler was still standing in the doorway, now shifting from one foot to the other like he was a toddler who had to go to the bathroom or someone who was inkling to dance, but didn't know how to go about it.

"You're getting on my nerves. What gives?" he asked.

"This woman is not just your ordinary everyday woman. She's special. I'm talking about the most beautiful woman in the entire world and guess what?" he asked.

Tyler was so excited, Kenneth had to find out.

"Okay, I'll play along. What?" he asked.

"She's here to see you and only you. Trust me you will not believe who she is. You better get out there because every man in this joint is crawling to get close to her and when you see her, you'll know why."

Kenneth was extremely curious now.

"She asked for me, specifically?"

"Yes."

"Did she say why?"

"No, but she didn't call you Cap or Captain Gibson like most people do around here. She's also not from around here. She called you Kenneth. It was really friendly like. She's a real beauty, Cap. I'm serious, you have to come out here and see for yourself."

"If this is some kind of practical joke, you're not going to like my response."

"Cap, just come see. I promise it's not a joke. It's a freaking Christmas wish come true, just not for us, but definitely for you."

Before he could ask Tyler any more question, Kenneth saw the doorway empty out as Tyler raced away.

Thinking it was a joke of some kind, he started to ignore the request until he heard so much ruckus coming from the truck bay that he had to go see what all the fuss was about. Something or someone had everyone riled up.

Leaving his office and rounding the corner, he could see a group of his firefighters gathered. There were so many men and women that he couldn't see who the object of their attention was in the center of them.

"Alright, what gives?" he asked walking up to them.

When the group quieted down and parted like the Red Sea had been in the movie classic, *The Ten Commandments*, in the midst of the mayhem was exactly as Tyler had described, the most beautiful woman in the world. It was Bella. She was here to see him.

Neither of them said a word as their eyes connected on more than just a casual level. It had been like that for them from the moment they met. That all changed three days ago, the last time he saw her in person. It wasn't a good parting and he wasn't sure of what brought her to him today. He expected to never see her in person again, at least until the movie release party in a year. He and Willow were invited to attend since she had a small part in the movie. He assumed that Bella would be halfway to Paris by now, taking Brandon back, yet again.

"Bella?" he asked.

He knew it was her, but he was still surprised and needed her to speak to know that she was real.

"Hi, Kenneth."

"Kenneth? Whoa, that sounds better than when she greeted us; sexy even," Tyler said.

Kenneth growled under his breath at every man who couldn't take his eyes off of her. He was feeling quite territorial over a woman who'd treated him like he never mattered to her, yet here he was about to clear the room.

"Go away. Everybody under the sound of my voice should step further away, right now or you'll all be cleaning the floors with toothbrushes next week. I do believe there are still boxes of bikes to be assembled and a few dollhouses, too. Get to it and let her breathe. I know it's cold outside but Bella doesn't need all your hot breaths breathing down on her."

To add to his point, Kenneth waved his hand in their direction as he walked toward them, giving everyone no option but to move away.

As they groaned with disappointment, each one of them waved at Bella and walked away. Kenneth stayed where he stood and took in a vision he missed seeing and holding in his arms.

"You're here?" he asked.

"I am. I came to see you."

She spoke so eloquently that Kenneth's heart

practically skipped a beat.

"How did you know where I'd be?"

Before she could answer, he looked around and saw at least a dozen sets of eyes on them, trying hard to listen and see everything happening. He grimaced at them before his crew finally turned and walked out of sight.

"They're funny," she giggled.

"They know a beautiful woman when they see one and of course, you're Bella. They've never had a celebrity here in their midst before. They don't know what to do. You know they were snapping picture after picture of you on their phones, right?"

Bella chuckled even more.

"I know and it's okay. I get that a lot."

"Even pictures of you with me?" he asked.

"Can we talk someplace private?" Bella asked.

"Yes, let's go in my office."

Kenneth turned and led them around a corner and into his office where he not only closed the door but he closed the blinds on the large glass window and the ones that covered the glass on the door. He was sure, given the chance, someone on his crew would find a reason to walk by his office just to see what was going on.

"This is nice. You even have a sofa in here. I love the beautiful mountainous view out of that large window behind your desk. I bet it's beautiful when it snows."

Kenneth pointed to the sofa where she took a seat while he leaned back against his desk, crossing his denim covered legs at the ankles. He wanted to sit with her but he was afraid he wouldn't be able to do so without pulling her into his arms. He needed to find out why she was here.

"It is and it will be in a couple of days. We're expecting about a foot of snow. It's the most beautiful sight of white, but no match to you looking strikingly beautiful in all white. I thought there was this thing of not wearing white after Labor Day?" he joked.

"That's for people who don't know how to think for themselves. I have my own mind and I wear any color any time of year. Besides, I love wearing white. Thank you for the compliment. You have a way of saying things and looking at me as if I'm the most beautiful sight you've ever seen. There is always so much desire in your eyes when you look at me," she said.

"Not enough, though, right?"

This was it, a change in the conversation He was anxious to get to the talk they should have had days ago, but he wasn't sure he was ready until now.

"Not true. That's why I'm here. I need to apologize and explain about that day."

"You don't have to. I understand. I'm not about that Hollywood drama."

"I know you're not and I'm so sorry. What I said is not what I was feeling. Will you allow me the chance to explain?"

"Of course," he said.

"I was striking back at Brandon for being who he has always been and who I have allowed him to be. I have had the worse choices in men, something I'm sure you already know. My life has been in the news, which I hate and that didn't become so relevant until that day. I didn't mean to say any of that. You mean everything, and I do mean, everything to me. You brought so much peace into my life; peace I didn't realize I needed. I've wanted it, but I've never fought hard to get it. Once my career took off, I allowed myself to become the Hollywood I never really wanted to be, at least not in how that life impacts me personally."

"Your words were brutal and my daughter heard them. Do you have any idea how long it took me to unwind her that evening? I won't even begin to tell you how deep those same words cut me. I went home telling myself I should have expected it. You are Bella Hardwick, the most sought-after Hollywood actress and here I am a local firefighter thinking we actually had a chance."

"Correction, the woman you know is CaBella Hardwick, not Bella. I had been giving you the real me. That's who you were with, not who you saw that day."

"What was I? A replacement in bed while you were here shooting your movie? Until you got back to Brandon? I can't even begin to see what you see in that guy. I can't say that I believe everything I see and read about this guy, but it's pretty wild, his behavior."

"Oh, you can believe it and so can I. What makes a woman continue her involvement with a playboy like him? I don't know. Brandon was easy. My schedule is crazy and so is his. People like seeing us together, but most of it was for the cameras."

"It was that day on-set as well. He had media people with him capturing his good side while he embarrassed you publicly. You should never settle for any man treating you that way; not in private and not in public. His lack of respect for you had me close to losing it. I wanted to land him flat on his ass, but I don't look good in prison stripes. What saved him from me was having Willow with me. I would never let her see me behave like a caveman, but I was close."

Kenneth laughed to himself. He could do that now, but that day, he was hot enough to not care about going to jail for knocking Brandon out. He was angry enough at the man's flippant treatment of Bella that he was willing to deal with the consequences even after hearing Bella say what she had.

Bella stood and walked closer to him. He still wanted to reach for her but instead, he gripped the edge of his desk tighter. He wasn't sure if he was getting the Bella who fell asleep in his arms or the actress on the screen. He was hoping for the first.

"You have no idea how sorry I am for what I said knowing I didn't mean not even a word of it. I didn't want to tell him what I felt for you. It was none of his business and it's still not."

"Weren't you supposed to join him in Paris? Wasn't that the invitation? Were you headed there before you came here?" he asked.

"No. I was headed to my home in Los Angeles to spend Christmas either alone or with a few friends who decided they weren't going to fly to visit their families for Christmas. My parents, as you know, are on holiday and my brother and his family are enjoying the holiday in Hawaii. He told me to come there, but I didn't want to. Even before I met you, I had no plans of joining Brandon in Paris. After meeting you, I wanted nothing more than to spend the holiday with you and Willow. I fell really hard for you, real fast. I know it may look like I do that a lot based on what you see and read, but that's not it at all," she confided.

"No?" he asked.

Kenneth was surprised at her revelation. The way the media portrayed her life, she was never without a man in her life.

"No. That's the truth. When you and I went back to your house that night and you made love to me, I have never, ever fallen in bed with a man that fast before. I know what you're thinking, but it's true. It took months when I was with Brandon and before him, the boyfriend I had was even longer than that. Before that guy, there was no one. All the men was all media hype of my agent and publicist. They wanted to build up that image of every man's dream woman, beauty, brains and can kick ass on the movie screen. None of that is me. You got the real me. I've never shown that to anyone before."

Kenneth searched Bella's face for truth and honesty and that's exactly what he saw. He saw a woman so vulnerable that she was willing to put her pride aside and lay her true feelings on the line. There was no doubt in his belief of her.

"Where does that leave us? What do you want? Do you know what you want? Because, see, I know what I want. It's what I've wanted since the moment I met you. I've wanted you from day one and that hasn't changed. I was angry, but seeing you right now, like this, I know you didn't mean what you said. I knew it all along, but that didn't stop the sting."

Bella smiled up at him, leaned forward with her head on his chest and wrapped her arms around his body, holding him tight.

Kenneth reached around her body and pulled her as close to him as he could. When she leaned back slightly, he lowered his head until their lips touched, lightly at first and then the passion, full of all the love he had for her spilled over and led to a deeper, more erotic, loving kiss. He missed this. He missed stolen moments like this. When she leaned back and smiled up at him, his entire world had just settled into the perfection it was meant to be with them.

"You have lipstick on your lips," Bella said, reaching up to wipe it off.

"I'll get it off before we step out of this room or we'll

be the talk of the firehouse for the foreseeable future. I'm in love with you, Bella. I know it sounds crazy after a few weeks and some serious steamy love sessions. I don't think I've ever had these kinds of deep feelings for any woman."

"What about Willow's mother?"

"I love her and I always will, but I can't say that I was ever, truly in love with her. I found that out because of the deep feelings I have for you. She and I met, dated and she got pregnant. We got married but realized we were better friends than spouses. You brought out a feeling of nesting that I've never experienced."

"With you, I was able to shut out the world and enjoy the moment. I'm usually ducking and dodging cameras and paparazzi who follow me everywhere. I appreciated how you were able to stunt on all of them and whisk me away to your house for privacy and peace."

"Did you bring paparazzi with you here?" he asked.

"Not at all. I used my stand-in again and switched hotels a few days ago. Using your tactic, I snuck out through a back entrance and my driver too me to your house. I didn't want to leave Maryland. I didn't want to leave you. The thought of leaving and not kissing you or making love to you again was frightening. You are what we women dream of. You're not fazed by my celebrity status. You treated me like CaBella, the woman my parents gave birth to and raised, not Bella, the actress or any character I play on the screen. For the first time, I turned my cell phone off with no need to look at it, check a message or look at my social media accounts. I was with you and Willow having the best time of my life. Remember when you made love to me and I cried?" she asked.

"I do."

"It was because I wasn't with a man making love to my character, you were loving me; you were seeing me. You see me now. I can see the difference in your eyes, in the way you talk to me, care for me, touch me. I have missed that the past few days. I was intent on not leaving here until we at least talked and if you didn't want anything to do with me, I would take it, but you would be hard to get over."

"What about Brandon? What about your life outside of me? Will we be distant buddies, friends, in a relationship? I live here in Maryland. You live in Los Angeles and anywhere else your movies are filmed. What do you want us to be? You know that Willow and I are a package deal in any and all situations. I'm her father first."

Kenneth needed to hear her say it. He was willing to do anything outside of moving from Maryland, to be with her. Willow was still his priority and nothing or no one could ever take him away from her.

"I love you and I love Willow," she explained.

"I love you, too."

"I have a career and I know your life is here. I want

to believe that we can have a relationship no matter where I am and that when I'm not wrapped up in my career, I can find my peace here in Maryland with you and Willow. I don't know what that will look like, but please tell me you'll try. I love what I feel like and who I am with you. I just want to be Bella who turns her phone off, curls up on the sectional with you and Willow and watch *Dreamgirls* a million times. As much as I love that movie, I've never enjoyed it more than singing every song and saying every word along with Willow. Do you question if we're compatible? Do you think I would be enough for you in a relationship?"

"Baby, you are enough for me in every way possible. I don't have any reservations about our compatibility. Does the age difference bother you?"

"Not one bit. I love that you're older. Clearly, you're the type of man I need and want because for three weeks, I've been happier than I have been since I became a woman. With you is where I want to be. The past few days, I've reflected on what I want in my life and in my career and I need both to fit together into a package that includes you and Willow. I love you. I love you so much. Thank you for showing me, in a few short weeks, that I'm enough without the fame. Thank you for seeing me and just me. I came here tonight because I want to fight for anything we can have as long as it includes many, many nights in your arms and much more fun times with you and Willow. Is what we shared so far enough for you to want more?"

Kenneth didn't hesitate.

"I want all of you and yes, I think we can have much more than what three weeks have shown us. Imagine how amazing we can be with more time together. We can work out the logistics of where the relationship goes as long as you know right here in my arms is where you will always find warmth, love and peace just as I find when I'm in your arms. No more drama, baby. We deserve more than that; you deserve more than that."

"Does that mean I can cancel my flight plans for tonight? I don't want to be in Los Angeles. I want to be with you. I want to send my family holiday greetings and then shut my phone off until I have to leave."

"When is that? How much down time do you have?"

"I don't start the press run for the movie until the summer. I was already planning on taking a break until then to spend time with family and take some much-needed vacations to wind down. I've been on a movie run for the past few years and I need a break. Would I outstay my welcome if I spend my time here?" "Here in Harford County, Maryland? Are you sure you won't get bored? Once the media discovers you're here, our lives are going to be crazy."

"Will that be too much for you?" she asked.

"Never. You can stay as long as you want. By the time you're back on the road this summer, perhaps I can get some time off and Willow will be out of school for the year. I'm sure I can convince her mother to let her travel with me as we travel around with you. That is, if you want our company."

Kenneth grew concerned when he saw tears stream down Bella's face.

"You would do that? You're making me cry. I don't know what to say."

"You're willing to give up your high-life to spend it here with us and when I can accommodate the schedule you have, I want to be there for you too. We're going to be in this together and that will mean sacrifices for both of us. I don't want cameras in Willow's face or following her around, so there is that to deal with. It's only a matter of you being out and about once for people to realize you are here, with me. We're going to look out and find cameras all over the place."

"I can take care of that with no problem. I have the best team and besides, I give interviews and stop for pictures with every media outlet. In return, I ask that I get private time with no cameras in my face. Once people find out about us, I'm going to beg them for my privacy while I'll also grant in-person interviews, especially for the local networks. I'm thinking for at least a month, I want to be as quiet as I can spending time with you cooking, watching movies and having date nights when we can get the proper disguises!" Bella quipped.

"I can get with that. The world will wonder where is Bella!"

"Let them wonder. Even if they find me, they'll get

tired of waiting when they realize I love spending my time doing nothing."

"You're serious, aren't you?"

"I won't be able to prevent your life being out in the open because you're the man I love. People are going to want to know you."

"I don't care what people want to know. I can grant interviews too, if that will keep people from trying to figure me out. I'm an open book. At least for the holiday, I get to have you to myself. Should we head back to my place and tell Willow?"

Kenneth had a renewed excitement that he didn't have when he arrived. He couldn't begin to imagine what his family will think when they see her at his house. He was expecting his parents, his sister and her family and Gabby and Ray for dinner on Christmas evening. He wouldn't tell them. He couldn't wait to see the shock on their faces.

"Actually, I would like to help out here. Is there anything I can do?" she asked.

"Ugh, that means no one else will get anything done. They'll be too busy watching you," Kenneth joked. "In all seriousness, that would be perfect. Willow will be asleep by the time we get there. I'll be able to put her toys out and then get in bed early."

"Ooh, that sounds like a perfect night. I'm going to need to go shopping for winter clothes. I wasn't expecting all this cold weather."

"I don't want you causing any stampedes at the

local mall. May I suggest on-line shopping while you're here until we can figure out how we'll handle the public? Besides, I want to be selfish and have you all to myself."

"That's a deal. Now, put me to work. I'm going to let my driver know he can go be with his family. I also need to get my luggage from him."

"I'll take care of the luggage. I think that and your driver can wait another five minutes. Once you go out to start helping, I won't have you to myself for the rest of the evening."

Bella snuggled closer to him, leaning up as close as she could to his lips. He didn't make her wait for what they both wanted. He took her lips in a hot, spicy kiss while slipping his hands inside of her coat to really feel her warmth.

Before the kiss got out of control, they heard a soft knock on the door.

"That was a quick few minutes!" Bella laughed.

Kenneth went to the door and snatched it open. He wasn't surprised to see Tyler on the other side.

"This better be good," Kenneth warned.

"Uh, yeah, it is. We're ready to deliver the bikes. We're starting to load them up on the truck. You have the final list of addresses and I need that."

"Okay. I want to come out and thank that team before you guys leave. I know it's a lot for Christmas Eve, but the kids are who matter."

"I agree, Cap. Also, you might want to wipe your

lips before you come out. Bella looks like she's been laying one or maybe two or three on you!" Tyler joked before slipping away, giggling like a little kid.

"I told you your lips are covered in red," Bella said.

Kenneth was about to grab a napkin from his desk when she grabbed it first and proceeded to wipe his lips.

"To be continued tonight?" he asked.

"Absolutely and every night after that. You have three days of kisses and other stuff to make up for."

"I got you covered, baby. I know we agreed no activities with Willow in the house, but if we're going to make a go of this, she'll have to get used to us being in the same bedroom. On the activity front, we can always take our party to the first-floor guestroom where you usually stay when you're at my house."

"Are you sure? Because I would like nothing more than to walk up every morning with your arms around me."

"I'm positive. We won't be rocking the bed or going crazy with my daughter in the house, but I'm sure it will be okay. I love you and that's something Willow will get used to quickly. She'll be happy."

"Whew! That's good because she wasn't happy with me earlier."

"She let you have it, huh?"

"She certainly did. Gabby made her apologize, but I understood her anger with me. I said some terrible things that she never should have been front and center for."

"That was Brandon's fault, not yours."

"Still, I never want to do anything to hurt her ever again. I want her to love me as much as I love her. I think she's forgiven me. I winked at her and she winked back just before I left."

"Well, wait until she hears that you're going to be staying with us for a while."

"Can I tell her?" Bella asked.

"You can do and have anything you want," he said snuggling closer.

"In that case, how soon before we wrap up here. I know what I want for Christmas."

"Oh?"

"Yes. I'll tell you my wish if you tell me yours."

"Baby, I have a feeling they are one in the same. Thanks for saving us. You didn't have to come here tonight, but I'm sure glad you did."

"I'll show you how happy I am a little later."

Kenneth took her by the hand and led her from the room."

"Let's hurry and get to that!" he shouted as they practically ran to join the others.

13
Christmas Morning

Bacon sizzled in the frying pan, grits boiled in a pot on the back burner while fried potatoes, onions and green peppers sizzled on another burner. Kenneth reached into the refrigerator for the fresh fruit he still needed to slice and place in the glass bowl he pulled from under the counter. Soft music played throughout the family room, dining room, living room and kitchen as he hummed along to the sultry sounds of Christmas from the Temptations while he prepared his version of a breakfast for champions. He was feeling especially grateful and happy, not just because it was Christmas morning, but because this was going to go down as one of his favorite Christmases of all time.

Looking toward his decorated kitchen table on the other side of the six-seat marble counter, he saw the slices of toast neatly stacked along with sliced bagels. There was a carafe of orange juice and one filled with chocolate milk. There was syrup for the French toast he was about to place on the griddle. He was ready to start the morning. Just as he was about to wonder why Willow hadn't popped up yet since she usually rose way before him on Christmas morning, she came bounding around the corner from the stairs and smiled up at him.

"Merry Christmas, beautiful one!" he chimed and picked her up in his arms, not caring he had pots cooking on the stove that he needed to watch. The most important aspect of his day was always her.

"Merry Christmas, daddy!" Willow sang in his ear as her arms gripped his neck tight. "You woke up before me!" she added.

"I know. I was about to go up and check on you. It's eight in the morning and usually you're up before the sun. You must have been tired last night," he said swinging her around, enjoying hearing her laughter as he did so.

"Godmommy helped me wrap your presents and that was a lot of work."

"You bought me even more presents?" he asked jokingly.

"Yes. Can we open them now?" she asked.

Kenneth sat her down on her feet and turned to check on the food.

"You know the drill. We always eat first and then we sit at the fireplace and open our gifts."

"Can I go see what Santa left me? He never wraps his gifts for me. I was an amazing daughter this year, wasn't I? I don't think Santa left me any coal."

Kenneth doubled over in laughter and kissed her forehead.

"There will never be any coal for you. There isn't a better daughter around anywhere who deserves all the gifts in the world more than you. Go ahead and look, but remember, you can't open your wrapped gifts until after breakfast."

"Okay, daddy," Willow said running off.

When he heard her shriek, he knew she saw her new bike, three different dolls, books, board games, movies, a new doll house and just as many clothes and accessories for her dolls as what Willow had in her own closet.

"Do you want sausage? I only made bacon so far," he stated loudly over her screams of joy.

"Daddy! Santa bought me a bike, a pink and white one! I got a great, big dollhouse, bigger than the one I got now."

"Have now," he corrected.

"Right, have now. I got new ice skates and roller blades. Santa brought me both, daddy! Yeah!" she declared from the other room.

Kenneth smiled. Nothing gave him more pleasure than Willow's happiness. It wasn't about spoiling her with things because they come and go. It was about being thankful that he could provide, not just her needs, but the things she wanted in life; especially at Christmas time.

"Looks like Santa was on his job, huh?"

"Yes! Thank you, Santa!" Willow yelled.

Kenneth smiled when she raced back into the kitchen.

"Sausage?" he asked again.

"Oh, yes. I want sausage and bacon. Do we have any ham?" she asked. "I like ham."

"Yes. I'll cook a little of that too."

When he turned back around to Willow, the big, bright smile on her face had disappeared. Her eyes suddenly appeared quite sad-like. He looked at her questionably.

"I like everything Santa brought me, but he didn't grant my wish for you. He didn't bring you a girlfriend," she said somberly.

He picked Willow back up on in his arms.

"I know you tried and it's okay."

"No, it's not okay. He brings me everything I ask him for that I want for me. It's my fault he didn't bring me what I wanted most for you. I didn't wish hard enough. Also, I was really mean to Miss Bella last night," she admitted, turning her eyes down as if she were ashamed.

He lifted her face back up to his.

"We don't hide our eyes or our feelings, right? When were you mean to Miss Bella last night?"

"She came over when me and godmommy were wrapping gifts. I told her that she was mean to you and I was mad. Godmommy made me apologize and I really am sorry, daddy. I didn't mean to be in grown people stuff like you always tell me. I thought she was going to be your girlfriend and I ruined everything by being mean. That's why Santa didn't give me my wish."

"He didn't?"

Kenneth smiled as Bella joined them in the kitchen. He watched Willow's head turn, almost in slow motion as the seconds ticked by before she realized who she was seeing.

"Willow?" Kenneth asked.

Before he knew what was going to happen next, Willow jumped from his arms and ran the few steps to Bella with speed as if she were on a racetrack.

"You're here!" she proclaimed and hugged Bella tight around the waist.

"Yes, I'm here. Where else would I be other than with you and your dad on Christmas morning."

"I thought you were leaving," Willow said.

"Leaving? Now, why would I do that?"

"Because I made a wish on our tree for Santa to make you daddy's girlfriend and then I was mean to you. I'm sorry."

"You said sorry last night and that was enough. Clearly Santa thought so too because here I am."

When Willow looked his way, Kenneth winked at her as he stirred the pot of grits.

"Are you daddy's girlfriend? Is that grown people stuff, daddy? Can I ask that?"

"It's okay to ask that," he assured her.

Willow turned back to Bella.

"Well?" she inquired.

"Yes, I am your daddy's girlfriend and I am as happy as a clam. This is the best Christmas ever and do you know why?" Bella beamed.

Kenneth watched the moment between his two favorite girls as Bella spoke.

"Why?" Willow asked.

"Because I love your daddy so much and I love you too. Guess what else?" Bella asked.

"What else?" Willow and Kenneth asked at the same time.

"When I was here watching movies with you and your dad and having a good time, he picked you up when you fell asleep and took you up to your room. While he was gone, I made a wish on your tree too."

"What did you wish?" Willow asked.

"I wished that Santa would make your daddy my boyfriend because I fell in love with him. Do you know that you have the most amazing, most remarkable, most loving dad in the whole world?"

"I do. My dad is the best; he's the greatest."

"Yes, he is and so I think that Santa heard your wish and he heard my wish and knew that me, you and your dad were meant to spend this Christmas holiday together. So, I'm here and I'm not going anywhere. Thank you for making your wish. I think we swamped Santa and he didn't have a choice but to make them come true. What do you think about that?" Bella asked.

Kenneth knew what he thought about it and to him,

this was the beginning of his own wish he'd made on the same tree. When he first laid eyes on Bella, he knew they were destined to be together. He wasn't sure it would have happened as fast as it did, but when something is right, it's right. He and Bella were perfect together.

"I love it! Don't you love it, too, daddy?"

Kenneth walked over and hugged them both.

"I love it a lot. I love you and I love you too, Bella. Merry Christmas," he said.

"Merry Christmas!" Willow shouted. "I love you, Miss Bella. I love you, daddy."

"Merry Christmas! I love you too, Willow, and Kenneth, thank you for being my wish come true."

"Daddy, can I show her what Santa left for me?"

"Yes. I need to finish breakfast. Gabby and Ray will be here shortly and they'll be hungry, as usual."

As they walked away from him, Kenneth chuckled at Willow's excitement.

"This is the best Christmas ever. Did I tell you that Santa ate all the cookies I left him and the glass of milk?" Willow asked Bella.

"Did he now? He must have loved it all. Show me what's under this magical tree," Bella said.

Kenneth winked at her just before they moved out of sight.

"How long are you staying?" Willow asked her.

"Until you get tired of having me here."

"That means you'll be here with me and my dad

forever!" Willow chimed.

"That works for me," Bella agreed.

"For me too!" Kenneth yelled from the kitchen.

"This is the best Christmas. Thanks to our tree, our wish was granted," Willow said.

"It was the best wish I could have ever made," Bella exclaimed.

"Me too," Kenneth declared to himself. This was his best year yet.

Epilogue
Christmas Eve – One Year Later

"Everyone, I want you all to meet my wife, Bella Hardwick," Kenneth said across the large room at the firehouse. The room full of kids and parents cheered as the kids made a mad dash for Bella who happily embraced as many of them as she could.

"Correction, my name is Bella Hardwick-Gibson and it's a pleasure meeting all of you," she said.

Kenneth leaned down and kissed her quickly on the lips as all the kids covered their mouths and some their eyes with embarrassment over his public display of affection for his wife. He still couldn't believe that she was married to him. He was going down in history as the luckiest man to ever live. The most beautiful girl in the world now carried his last name.

He was still on cloud nine three months after their wedding on the beach in Hawaii. His family, including Carrie, her husband, and their daughter Sapphire, were in attendance along with close and other extended family. He thought Bella would want to invite her celebrity friends, but she decided against it. She wanted the day to be about family and close friends, allowing her family the time to get to know his. Of course, Willow was front and center and served as the flower girl for the ceremony. Gabby, Ray and Bella's brother, Sean stood with him while Desiree, Dana and his sister, Lindsay, stood with Bella. They were married as the sun went down, making for an enchanted evening.

Bella had worn a long white gown as she walked barefoot to him on the sand where he stood in his gray tuxedo welcoming her into his life forever. He didn't feel less of a man when he couldn't control the tears that flowed as soon as he saw her. They had spent months having a relationship that everyone dreams of having. There was never a doubt that the next step for them was getting married.

After the wedding, they danced the night away until he could enjoy the best part of the evening with Bella in his arms in their private suite. Willow spent the rest of the week with her mother while he and Bella flew to Bali for their honeymoon. Spending a week in paradise doing nothing but loving each other was the real Shangri-La, their own private utopia.

Tonight, they were back in Maryland after a quick trip to their home in Los Angeles where family had joined them for Thanksgiving a few weeks back. They were now at the firehouse for the annual toy drive.

Later, he would join other men to put together bikes and other toys that needed assembling, something he took part in every year.

"This is Chief Eddie. He runs this house. Everyone else, you can introduce yourselves."

He smiled when Gabby and Ray walked over to him smiling like two giddy little kids.

"Hey Bella!" Gabby said greeting her with a hug.

"Hey lady! I'm so happy to see you. I thought you were coming by the house earlier. I baked," Bella admitted.

"You baked? As in cooked? What did you cook or bake?"

"Godmommy, we baked cookies! We made three kinds and Bella baked a cake that is delicious. Guess what kind?" Willow asked jubilantly.

"Lemon!" Gabby yelled.

"Yes, my favorite!" Willow saluted with a high-five.

"It was good?" Gabby questioned.

"Yes, and we saved you a big slice."

"Well, I guess that means me and uncle Ray will have to come by before we go home. I have a hankering for some good lemon cake. Why don't you go help give out the toys to the little kids and let me talk to your daddy and Bella," Gabby stated.

After Willow ran off, Kenneth felt himself and Bella being pulled into another room by Gabby with Ray in tow.

"What gives?" he asked.

"First of all, I'm happy you're spending Christmas in Maryland. I know you were thinking of going back to Los Angeles since you have the week off. What changed your minds?"

"Carrie wasn't expected to have her baby until New Year's Day and Willow was going to spend Christmas at home. She had the baby yesterday, surprise, surprise and we decided Willow should come with us and give Carrie a break. I wanted her to still be close to family for Christmas. Believe it or not, it was Bella's idea. She's turning in to a Marylander! She's decided to make here her home base."

"I love it here. It's where I met the man who showed me what real love is. Besides, I made a promise that if God and Santa gave me back my man for Christmas, I would do everything in my power to make our love last a lifetime and that means compromise."

"Don't you have a movie to jet off too?" Ray asked.

"Not for another six months. Until then, I'm planning to live the domesticated life with my man and my step-daughter baking and all that good stuff. We also plan to start working on making a little Gibson addition to our family," Bella added.

"A baby? You want to have a baby?" Gabby asked.

"Yes. We are actively, and I do mean very actively, working on it. Now, like Kenneth said, what's the deal? Is everything okay?"

When Gabby looked to Ray and then back to him, Kenneth thought something was wrong at first. Then he saw a big stupid smile on Gabby's face and knew whatever was about to happen was good news.

"Ray?" Gabby said, turning to him.

"Okay. Gabby and I have decided to get married," Ray said.

Gabby then flipped her hand at them and Kenneth picked her up, spun her in the air before placing her back on her feet. Hugs went all around with excitement.

"That's not all," Gabby said.

"Okay, I'm ready. What can be better than that?" Kenneth asked.

"My cousin, Sheria, agreed several months ago to be a surrogate for me and Ray and yesterday, a Christmas miracle happened just in time for Christmas tomorrow. She called to tell us that she's pregnant, three months. I'm going to be a mommy!" Gabby cheered.

Kenneth was so happy that he again picked her up and this time danced around with her in his arms. When he set her down, everyone was crying with happiness. He had hoped that the fact that Gabby couldn't have her own children didn't mean that she couldn't still have children of her own.

"You have no idea how happy that makes me. I've always wanted children for you. I've seen you with Willow and I knew you would be a fantastic mother. This is wonderful news."

"Well, I figure, if Bella can put out a wish for you,

and Willow could put out a wish for you and Bella, I would try my hand to see if Santa was really granting wishes. Seems like it's a good move. I'm going to come by tonight and then tomorrow, Ray and I are going to visit his parents in D.C. I had to tell you first. You've always been there for me since that day on the school bus. I can't wait for you to meet either your godson or goddaughter. I already know Bella is going to be the perfect godmother."

"Me? You want me to be the godmother?" she asked.

"Yes, you and Carrie will share that responsibility along with Ray's sister. His brother-in-law, Tyler and Carrie's husband will share in godfather duties along with Kenneth. I need all love around this baby at all times. What it has taken for me to get to this is nothing but a miracle that only Santa could make happen."

"I'm so happy. Now, we will have to go back to the house and eat cake!" Bella cheered.

"That sounds like a great plan. Ray and I are going to go finish with the toy giveaway."

After they walked off, Bella was about to follow them and Kenneth pulled her back into the small room and shut the door.

"Mr. Gibson, what are you doing? There are families out there. People will be looking for us," Bella exclaimed the moment he pulled her into his arms. The passionate kiss silenced all conversation for at least a minute until he gave her air to breathe.

"Is that an answer for you?" he questioned about the powerful kiss.

"That's always the right answer for me," she declared.

"How many babies do you want?" he asked.

"A lot."

"A lot?"

"Yes, a lot. I never thought of myself as anyone's mother, but being married to you and a second or third mother to Willow after Gabby, of course, I now realize how much I want a brilliant, beautiful little girl like her or a strikingly handsome little boy like his daddy running around."

"What about your career?"

"My career is secondary to my life with you and our family. Do you know that I no longer care about making more millions on top of the millions I already have? I couldn't spend it in a lifetime if I tried. The money will be there and the movie roles will be too. I want time to focus on you and having our babies. I want to build our family and many, many more Christmases like last year and this year. This is what life and love is all about. It's about family. You know I made that wish to have you in my life and when it came true that night I came to see you here at the firehouse, I knew that the only priority would be our love."

"That's exactly what I want. I only want you and our kids snuggled up in the family room."

Kenneth didn't think life could ever be this

wondrous. Bella was his dream girl come true. The life they were planning means everything to him.

"With lots of popcorn with hot sauce," Bella joked.

"I don't understand how you let Willow talk you into trying that and now you can't stop eating it. Are you sure you're not already pregnant?" he asked.

There was a time that Bella wouldn't touch hot sauce on popcorn and now, she eats it even when Willow isn't with them.

Bella didn't say anything in response but she did smile which made him wonder even more.

"Let's just say that I think Gabby won't be the only new mother in the new year. I bought a test. I want to take it with you in the room. Can we do it tonight?" she asked.

"Oh, baby!" Kenneth yelled and picked her up like he'd done Gabby, though he didn't put Bella back down on her feet. Instead, he wrapped her legs around his waist and feasted on her luscious lips.

"I take it that's a yes?"

"No doubt. Let me toss a quick wish up to Santa to put a baby under our tree for next Christmas. He seems to really like our family and friends."

"Then I'm quite sure Willow won't be the only child calling you daddy real soon."

"Wishing upon a star isn't the way to go anymore. It's wishing on a tree for Santa to grant said wish that works!" Kenneth said.

"I'm glad it worked for us."

"Merry Christmas, baby," Kenneth uttered before kissing her one last time.

"Merry Christmas, my love," Bella responded.

~~

Check out the first book in a new romantic series, "*Sister Act*", with book one, *An Unexpected Destiny*!

Preorder your copy today at www.cherylbarton.net

An Unexpected Destiny

Destiny Lockhart's high school crush, Lincoln Cole, is again front and center in her life. She last saw him fifteen years ago when she threw him out of her bedroom after their one night together following the senior prom. That night had been her most embarrassing moment, leaving her feeling ashamed and undesirable.

There was no way entertainment mogul Lincoln Cole could ever forget the shy, yet beautiful butterfly that was Destiny from his years as a high school football star. The now feisty, sexy and self-confident executive who dripped in vibrant, dazzling appeal reminded him that they were never meant to only have a one-night-stand. They were always destined for forever.

For years, they lived on two different coasts unaware that soon, their past would become an unexpected present filled with unfinished desires that once looked like rejection.

What's Coming Up Next?

It Should Have Been You

Dr. Clayton Myers was never a believer in karma, but he did believe in fate. Both would soon collide and expose a secret that would impact the perfect life and relationship with the only woman he ever loved, but not the only woman he took to his bed. That revelation would put his life on a path he accepted while never forgetting what could have been.

Dr. Donna Spencer had experienced one of the darkest days of her life at the hands of the man who had made a promise of forever to her. She took the hit to her heart and realized nothing good lasts forever.

After years of no contact, Clayton and Donna's paths would cross again, forcing them to face the past while wondering what should have been.

The Christmas Layover

A Novella – Early 2022 Release

Millionaire Edrick Stone's plan to spend the Christmas holiday alone at his villa in Spain was derailed by a sudden snow storm that hit Denver, Colorado just as he was leaving. He couldn't be mad at the storm when he discovered friendly passenger across the aisle was also stranded, much to his delight.

Danica hated Christmas; even her friends secretly called her Scrooge. She carried a secret pain that resurfaced each year with the holiday until a mysterious stranger on a plane offered her the chance to have a very merry Christmas. She decided to throw caution to the wind and live in the moment.

Edrick and Danica had their own reasons for avoiding Christmas, but this year, they would find that the holiday wasn't meant to be spent alone, but in arms filled with love and possibilities.

Book 3 of "The Sullivans of Montana"
Coming April 2022

On the Right Track

Dayton Sullivan is the youngest of the Sullivan boys and has found himself in a bit of a jam when he falls in love with Kima McDonald, the daughter of a man who could be responsible for the death of Kima's mother, the woman whose fortune Kima now holds in her hands that her father wants to gain control of.

Dayton and Kima run off to the Sullivan Ranch in Montana in order to escape the life she's being told she has to live according to her father's schemes.

Can their love sustain them through the ups and downs they'll face against her sinister father or will and those he is indebted to find a way to get Dayton back on the race track and Kima married to a man she doesn't love, but who holds all the cards when it comes to her future?

Check out these other recently released books from Cheryl Barton available at www.amazon.com/author/cherylbarton and www.cherylbarton.net

Seize the Moment

Aubree Campbell played a childish game with love and she lost. Ending her relationship with her live-in boyfriend, Russell Hall, because they became passing strangers in the night didn't have him begging and pleading for her to give him a second chance as she had hoped. Instead, the indomitable Russell made plans to move out and give her the space she desired and then a world pandemic hit and they agreed to ride it out together under one roof.

Tensions brewed and so did their undeniable desire and passion for one other. Will their steamy nights lead them back to being on the same page in life and in love or will past hurt and jealousy return to put an end to their rekindling?

The Power of Seduction

Bakery owner, Raquel Hastings, assumed her relationship was perfect in every way, both in and out of the bedroom where she had enjoyed the most tempting, titillating, and out-of-this-world sensual romps between the sheets with sexy engineer, Preston Sharpe, a man who knows his way around a woman's body. That was until he took a job in another country which left her only with memories and intoxicating desires to be loved like that again. Her world had been turned upside down until the day he returned with a plan to turn her world right side up.

Preston's alluring visions of Raquel haunted him at night, alone in his bed in a foreign country without the woman he loved. With the chance to return home and to her loving arms, he dreamed of once again sharing nights of satiating passion that only two hearts meant for each other could share. He knew he had to ready his game of seduction if he were ever going to again have Raquel back in his life and in his bed. This time, his plan was to make it last forever with the hope that Raquel could forgive him and give their love another chance.

Unforgettable

Baltimorean Reagan Kelly was expecting an uneventful weekend in New York City visiting her sister between Thanksgiving and Christmas. Though in the holiday spirit, the last thing she thought she'd find on a cold, wintery night was a chance at romance.

Two days in New York City for business and a chance to see his best friend was all Crime Novelist, Keith Jackson had time for, or so he thought. He soon found time to extend his stay when the chance of a lifetime to spend four incredible days with the most beautiful woman he'd ever encountered landed at his feet. An unforgettable weekend is one thing, but can that weekend turn into a lifetime of unconditional love for Reagan and Keith, two self-professed workaholics, who didn't have a reason to slow down and smell the roses until now?

Baby Come Back

Meridian, Mississippi, held nothing but bad memories for Sumaria Moore. Not only did she lose her parents who raised her in the southern city, but the love of her life had walked out on her three years ago, leaving not only their love behind, but a secret he never knew about.

Preston Washington wanted more than what a small, southern city could offer him. In order to make his dreams come true, he had to leave the only life he knew and the only woman he's ever loved.

A bad decision took them away from each other and then a tragedy brought them once again to the city neither wanted to go back to. Sumaria and Preston will soon find that the best kept secrets aren't the ones that are kept hidden; they are the ones that can show them how everything they left behind, could lead them to what they thought they once had; forever.

The Way You Love Me

Montana ranch owner, Perry Sullivan, befriended a woman who finds herself in dire need of his help. He doesn't hesitate to provide shelter and protection the way any man should for a woman who is in distress. What he had not planned on was in the midst of the turmoil that was her life, he would lose his heart and fall in love while at the same time putting the lives of his own family at risk.

Gizelle Duncan had a tumultuous past she didn't want anyone to know about, but when that past, in the form of her abusive ex-husband, shows up in her life again, she has no choice but to accept help from one of those sexy Sullivan boys from the Sullivan Ranch. She thought she had lost all faith in real love until Perry showed her that she could trust him not only with her life, but with her heart.

"The Way You Love Me" will take you on a journey from the ashes of Gizelle's burned-out house and life and into the flames of passion that will not be contained even at the peril of a jealous ex-husband out for revenge.

About the Author

Cheryl Barton lives in Maryland and in her spare time, she loves to read espionage, crime and romance novels, cook, watch Sci-fi movies, spend time with family and friends and enjoy Maryland steamed crabs.

Cheryl is celebrating over 30 years as a government employee and loves writing romance novels in her downtime. Her catalogue boasts over thirty romance novels and eight inspirational novels.

Cheryl was a 2019 Finalist for the Emma Award given by Romance Slam Jam and a 2018 Finalist for the Literary Trailblazer of the Year award by the Indie Author Legacy Award.

Indulge in more romance and inspirational novels by visiting her website at www.cherylbarton.net and make sure you connect with Cheryl on Facebook, Twitter and Instagram @cherylbartonbooks.

Check out other releases at www.cherylbarton.net. While you're there, join the list serv for information on upcoming releases, free novels and other giveaways.

www.ingramcontent.com/pod-product-compliance
Lightning Source LLC
Chambersburg PA
CBHW050520260626
47157CB00004B/1407
* 9 7 8 1 9 4 8 9 5 0 5 9 6 *